GUILIANO IMPORTS
A Erotic Tale of Satisfaction Guaranteed

First Edition

Published by The Nazca Plains Corporation
Las Vegas, Nevada
2010

ISBN: 978-1-935509-78-3

Published by

The Nazca Plains Corporation ®
4640 Paradise Rd, Suite 141
Las Vegas NV 89109-8000

PUBLISHER'S NOTE
Guiliano Imports is a work of fiction created wholly by *Bill Smith*'s
imagination. All characters are fictional and any resemblance to
any persons living or deceased is purely by accident. No portion of
this book reflects any real person or events.

Cover Photos
Raisa Kanareva and Valeriya Repina

Art Director
Blake Stephens

DEDICATION

To all those whose fantasies allow them one of life's greatest joys - a life of total satisfaction and fulfillment through the abundant use of slaves.

GUILIANO IMPORTS

A Erotic Tale of Satisfaction Guaranteed

First Edition

Bill Smith

PART I

"Guiliano Imports" the deep voice answered the phone.

"I... I... was given your number by a good friend of mine who... who... who has had some business dealings with you," I stuttered not knowing quite what to say.

"Who was this friend?" the voice replied suspiciously. "We'll need to know. We only do business with customers who we are sure of," he added coldly.

"Sure of?" I asked. "In terms of credit or character?" I shot back rather astonished.

"Both," he answered without emotion, but then added, "some of our transactions require a certain amount of discretion as well as confidentiality in order to protect our clientele."

"John Morgan gave me your number. He had purchased some items from you a few months ago."

"We've dealt with John for several years now," the voice brightened a little. "I'm Eduardo Guiliano, the old man's son. Are you interested in purchasing items in the same category as Mr. Morgan?"

"Yes, definitely, but our tastes are a little different. I understood through him you'll need to check my credit before we get too far."

"You got that right, Mr...?"

"Parsimi. Guilo Parsimi, Italian, like you. That's spelled P-A-R-S-I-M-I and the account number at Suisse Credit is 43808821.

"First name G-U-I-L-O?" Eduardo replied. "My secretary can validate your account on another line while we're talking, but I'll need to check this out with John Morgan. No offense - it's just we've got to be careful to protect our clients."

"I understand."

"I'll get back with you as soon as I get ahold of Mr. Morgan. If you don't hear from me, we're not interested in doing business. What's your number?

I gave Mr. Guiliano my number and hung up.

The next day the phone rang.

"Eduardo Guiliano here, Mr. Parsimi. Sorry it took so long but I couldn't get a hold of Mr. Morgan until late last night. He recommended you most highly as a potential customer and assured us you would not only be discrete but could afford anything you wanted. Suisse Credit more than confirmed that appraisal I might add. Looks like we're in business. If you're still interested, I need to get some general parameters of what you might be interested in now and we can work out the details later."

"Well, Mr. Guiliano. I'm looking for at least eight males, all around 18-20 years old, all about the same height and physique, muscular, but with different skin and hair colors. Also," I hesitated, "all should be very masculine, if you know what I mean."

"Yes, I know exactly what you mean, Mr. Guiliano. Any particular nationality?"

"No."

"Do they have to speak English?

"No."

"And I assume you want them pre-trained?"

"What does that mean?"

"Trained to accept the reality of their status in life now."

"Yes - they'll need to be thoroughly trained. I don't have the time, knowledge, or energy to get involved with all that."

"Well, Mr. Parsimi. I've got good news. We can meet your request and then some if you're willing to pay the price which will be pretty steep on stock like that."

"I'll pay if you deliver what I want," I assured him.

"In that case, the best thing to do is pick and choose yourself. That's the only way you're really going to be satisfied. We could pick some out for you, but beauty is in the eye of the beholder, they say, and our experience has certainly shown that's true. We can present a wide variety of offerings and you simply pick out those who suit your needs best."

"Sounds good. When and where?" I replied enthusiastically.

"Where do you live?" Mr. Guiliano asked.

"The mother country - Italy - Mr. Guiliano."

"You're in luck. We maintain one of our warehouses on a small unnamed island near Delos in the Aegean where we own the whole island for privacy. You go to Delos and we'll pick you up in our boat and take you over to our island. When you get to Delos, tell them where you're at - either the small landing strip there or the dock. Just call 08-881-5644-012 and in 20 minutes we'll be there to pick you up. Once you're on our own island, you'll be our guest so you don't need to worry about accommodations - we'll take good care of you and get you back to Delos whenever you like. But, Mr. Parsimi - you'll probably want to stay at least overnight. Selecting stock can be tiring, especially after a long trip."

"Sounds good. I can get to Delos in just a few hours from here by chartered plane. But how do I get my purchases back here to my estate?"

"Oh," Mr. Guiliano laughed, "let us worry about that. We're experts at shipment. We'll have them at your estate within 48 hours and all charges are included in the purchase price."

"Sounds great. Give me that phone number again. I'm looking over my schedule and I'm free day after tomorrow. I'll get a plane out of here on that morning. Should be at this airstrip you were talking about no later than noon day after tomorrow."

"I'll set it all up. Your contact there on our island is Arista Mythos - I'm sure you'll find him a charmer and he'll handle all the details for you - that's his job."

The small charter landed around 11:00 A.M. and I called the number given me on my cell phone. So far everything was going as smoothly as John Morgan had assured me it would. When the phone answered, it was Arista Mythos himself who told me one of his staff was already at the air strip to pick me up.

"Look for a young man around 25 or so driving a white BMW," he chuckled.

I looked around and sure enough, rapidly approaching me was a white BMW driving right up next to the plane. A strikingly handsome man leaped out, asking "Mr. Parsimi?"

"Yes," I replied as he quickly took my overnight bag from the pilot and put it in the luggage compartment and just as quickly opened the back door for me.

Within seconds we were speeding away from the airstrip down a dusty two lane road.

"It will only take us five minutes or so to get to the boat," he explained pleasantly.

"What do you do with the car?" I asked, curious if this was his only job.

"We just leave it locked up at the dock. We just use if for trips back and forth to the airstrip and a little sightseeing if a client wants to see the sights of Delos. You interested in seeing Delos?"

"Not now. I was here years ago but never knew there was another island nearby. I didn't see anything from the ship I was on at that time."

"No," he replied. "The shipping and air routes are all on the north side of the island. Our little island lies to the southeast and is far enough away you really can't see it from Delos, even on a clear day. Out of the way doesn't quite describe it," he laughed.

"Guiliano Imports owns the whole thing?" I asked.

"Yes. Only a few real old fishermen lived there when they bought it and they promptly all moved to the mainland once they had a few coins in their pocket. They were so old they're all dead now and everyone has forgotten the place ever existed. I tell the guys at the dock we're from Mithia, another island about 25 miles west of Delos. They view Mithia as the end of the earth, so they just tease me a little about having to live there and never ask questions."

"How did you end up living here?" I asked.

He stared at me briefly and then realized I was really clueless.

"No one asked me about it," he smirked as he reached up and pulled down his turtleneck sweater until I saw a bright metal collar fastened tightly around his neck. "I was shipped to the island in one of Guiliano Imports' own boats a number of years ago."

"But you speak Italian perfectly," I exclaimed, somewhat embarrassed that I hadn't figured out that Guiliano Imports obviously used their own products in lieu of regular employees.

"I should. I'm Italian, but I also speak enough English, German, Russian, Spanish, Arabic and a little bit of Chinese to be able to do my job."

"Well trained," was my only comment.

"Yes, but not just in languages," he winkled suggestively. "There's a quiet alcove right off the road up here if you're interested."

"Yes, very well trained," I laughed, "but I'll wait until we're at the company's island if you don't mind. That's a rain-check, not a 'no'," I chuckled, "if you look as good out of your clothes as you do in them."

"Yes... Master," he replied with a beguiling look, as he carefully again covered his collar with the turtleneck sweater top. "I don't want the dock workers to think I'm a hippie or something," he chuckled in explanation. "We keep the island's affairs totally private."

It turned out the boat was equipped with an autopilot so I didn't have to wait to get to the island to take my guide up on his invitation. Even though he was a beautiful man clothed, he looked even better out of his clothes than in them and was as skilled in the use of his body in pleasing me as he was in his mastery of languages. Within 15 minutes he had drained me dry and I just lay there studying his naked very muscular body. Not only was his neck collared, but he sported a small "G" brand on his right pectoral, both of his prominent brown tits had been fitted with 2" brass rings, and his genitals were banded with a thick collar of their own made of the same material as his neck collar and tit rings. The latter appliance forced his package out in front of him and not only emphasized its large size, but made it extremely easy to handle.

"You're something to behold," I commented as I twisted the band around his genitals a little, noting it was tightly welded. "Are all of Guiliano's products decked out like this?"

"Most," the boy answered, "but it can be removed easily if the customer wants it differently. Master Mythos thinks we sell better this way."

"And the brand?"

"We've all got that. Guiliano Imports brands all their stock. Reminds us of what we are, of course, and then Guiliano is proud of his products too," the boy reflected.

"You remember being branded?" I asked.

"It was the turning point of my life, seems like," the boy answered without malice. "After that, I realized I'd never be free or anything like that again so I might as well make the most of it."

"The most of it?" I queried.

"Well, you know, adjusting to what is - getting treated decently, making myself of some use to those who were now in charge, avoiding punishments, pleasing my owners - you know - that soft of stuff that all slaves have to deal with. What I didn't realize was the rest of it?"

"The rest of it?" I prompted.

"At that time, I didn't realize slaves take pride in what they do just like anyone else. But I soon caught on and took advantage of the opportunities offered me. I've learned a lot since then and am really proud of how much I have accomplished in just a few years. Learned all those languages, can please most anyone in bed, and am proving I'm a darn good overseer that can be trusted. That's more than I'd learned in my whole stinking life up until I came here. Now I'm a trusted and valued member of the organization that gives me a lot of pride inside."

You could have accused the boy of hubris, but it didn't come off that way. He seemed genuinely pleased that it had all worked out so well and that, even though he was now a piece of property owned by Guiliano Imports, he had gotten further in life than he ever thought possible, thanks to them. You definitely got the impression he thought the trade-offs in personal freedoms had been well worth it. But then, I reflected, we Italians are always ones to take advantage of the opportunities presented us.

Since the island was in sight, I expected the guide to put his clothes back on, especially since some of my cum was oozing out of his ass and down one of his thighs for all the world to see. But instead, he carefully folded his clothes and placed them in a small locker in the pilot's compartment before turning the autopilot off and guiding the boat neatly into the moorings while remaining stark naked.

When I looked at his bare body rather pointedly, he explained.

"Even the overseers are nude on the island, master. It's one of the Guiliano rules. Only Mythos and the guests like yourself are clothed. After all, we are a training and sales facility," he added as if all of this was self-explanatory and made perfectly good sense.

"In which case, I better get my duds on unless I want to be mistaken for a Guiliano property," I chuckled.

The guide laughed. "Don't worry, master. We'd know the difference. You're not collared."

"No," I laughed back. "But I hope there's more difference than that."

"Oh, there is, master," the guide replied with great respect. "You're obviously a person of great wealth and resources or you wouldn't be a guest here. The rest of us had only our bodies as assets and now, even those belong to Guiliano or whoever buys us. We've learned there is a natural order in the world, just like Aristotle claimed. Those who are masters and those who are slaves. Destiny has placed you as a master - fate has cast me as a slave. Both of us have to adjust to what is!"

"You're more Greek than Italian," I laughed. "But I agree with your philosophy. It makes for a happier world all around."

"Yes, master," the guide said with humility as the boat docked and he leaped out with my overnight bag and led me up a small stone path to the main facility still stark nude with a proud posture to him.

"Welcome to our island, Mr. Parsimi." A nice looking middle aged man stepped forward and shook my hand firmly. "Aristo Mythos here at your service. I see Santos got you over from Delos OK," Mythos said as he gently patted the bare rump of the collared slave who had served as my guide and, noting some stickiness, wiped his hand off in Santos' hair. "From the looks of things, he has been appropriately hospitable," he laughed as he wiped some cum off of Santos thigh and again wiped that off in the slave's hair.

I blushed at his brashness.

"No need to be embarrassed, Mr. Parsimi," he said assuredly. "That's exactly why you're here, isn't it? To pick out some stock for your pleasure?"

"Well, yes, but I hadn't counted on being treated to some of your offerings on the boat ride over," I shot back. "I thought I'd at least have to buy them first."

"Nonsense, Mr. Parsimi. You're our guest here and all the slaves are available at all times. It's part of their reality."

"Am I your only guest right now?" I asked.

"No, we've got a young man from Moscow with us. But he's not buying. He just supervised the delivery of 25 new boys from Russia he'd acquired and sold to us. He'll be leaving in the morning now that his stock is safely in our hands for extensive training. But he's an interesting person and I'm sure you'll enjoy his company when you get a chance. He's been in the business for about two years now and has some fascinating tales to share about acquiring some of his stock. He doesn't speak a word of anything but Russian, but Santos can act as your interpreter. Would you like to freshen up before looking over some of the available stock?"

"Yes, I probably need a shower after enjoying your initial hospitality," I replied as I looked pointedly at the cum still running down Santos' legs.

"Let Santos help you. He needs a shower himself from the looks of it. Santos, take Mr. Parsimi to Suite #1 and serve as his body servant."

"Yes, Master Mythos," Santos said as he again grabbed my overnight and led me a short distance away to a lovely guesthouse whereupon he carefully undressed me, administered a thorough shower with him scrubbing my back and massaging my legs and lower back, then toweling me down gently and carefully unpacking my overnight before offering himself once again for my enjoyment if I so desired.

"Not right now, Santos," I chuckled. "Later."

Santos promptly helped me dress and then stood to one side with his head bowed, obviously waiting for my instruction.

"I can rest later. Let's go see some of that stock your master was talking about."

"Yes, master," Santos said cheerfully, as he opened the door and motioned for me to follow him.

———————

As we entered the nearby warehouse, Santos picked up a whip on a table near the door looking amazingly like a British riding crop. The large facilities were clean, airy, and well organized with individual cages all along the perimeter of the building as well as alongside three low aisles dividing the area into sections. Since the cages were small - only about 4 x 4 x 4, they were stacked three high everywhere so overall I would judge there must have been at least 300 cages available. It looked like a good two-thirds of them were occupied.

"This is the stock that's completed training and are waiting for a buyer," Santos explained. "We're plenty well stocked right now, although, as you can see, we can house a lot more here. It all depends on sales and the number coming out of training at any given time. These properties have been here a short while - we haven't had too many buyers visiting us lately. All the others are in one or another of the training facilities."

"How many there?" I asked.

"With the 25 Russians delivered today, that should bring us to around 1668 in one stage of training or another. But training takes a while - usually 6 months to a year until they're really marketable, so you've got to have that many in training if you plan to have many sales offerings at any given time. Right now, the mix is about right. This gives the customer a good choice without giving us a serious surplus of stock on hand. Master Mythos told me you're interested in male stock around 18-20, well built, and heavy hung. He also said you wanted them about the same height and body build, but in different colors. Is that correct, master?"

"That's about it, Santos. I might as well tell you exactly what I'm looking for. I want eight litter-bearers who can tote a heavy litter all day long, have the endurance to run with that litter for considerable distances, look like a matched team in terms of how they're built - but in different skin and hair colors to make the team interesting to look at. They'll all have to be able to easily lift a heavy load and carry that load all day long if necessary, sometimes at a fast trot, so they'll have to have the muscles and wind to make that possible without too much fuss. They're as much for show as anything, so they're usually not going to be wearing much while serving as litter slaves and nothing at all when they're serving me in the privacy of my estate so they've got to have nice-looking bodies and be handsome in their appearance. In the evening, they'll be waiting table and servicing me and my guests with what their bodies have to offer and I don't want to be embarrassed in front of my guests by their deportment in that area so they'll need to be well trained in that area."

"Anything else, master?" Santos said humbly, totally unperturbed by my request as if everyone asked for this or something very similar.

"Well, I certainly like your rings and banding and think they would look good on my team. I assume they've already been branded with the Guiliano trademark and collared?"

"Yes, master. They're all branded, of course, but their collar is generally replaced with something a little nicer than their training collars which are just a loose heavy hinged iron collar with a padlock. Most owners like to install a good tight brass or copper collar that's welded on them permanently. And, if you want, we can tit ring and genitally band your purchases right here before you leave. May I suggest their collar match their rings and banding - gives a nice coordinated look, if I may say so, master," Santos said with lowered eyes.

"Santos, does that band around your genitals give you any trouble? It sure shows you off well."

"At first, master, it felt mighty strange and sort of threw me off balance, but I got used to it within a few days and barely notice it now. But it took my tit rings a good two weeks to heal and a good six weeks before I wasn't aware of them all the time. Even now, master, they're mighty noticeable to me - change in temperature, the wind hitting them, bouncing up and down when I walk or run. I'm not sure a slave ever gets totally used to them, master."

"A constant reminder, huh, Santos?"

"That and my collar, master. A slave never forgets they're collared, especially when they're fitted tight like this. You always know you're a slave," he smirked. "No way to forget that fitted out like I am."

"Is that good or bad, Santos?"

"Oh, it's good, master. Keeps me focused on what I am now."

"That's good to hear, Santos. I wanted the fittings for pure decoration, but I see they have deeper implications than just a mere decoration."

"Much deeper, master. They're like a brand in that respect."

"Well, let's see what you've got on hand," I said as I rubbed my hands together in anticipation.

"Your timing is good, master," Santos smiled. "The slaves have just finished their daily four hours of exercises followed by their routine cleaning and grooming procedures. With this many stock in one room, you begin to smell all those bodies by late evening."

Without further ado, Santos quickly disappeared into the maze of cages. I heard some cage doors creak open as the locks were undone, bare feet jumping down to the floor with those caged on the top rows, and a few grunts as the objects to be scrutinized stretched out their cramps from their confinement in the tiny cages. Within five minutes, 15 handsome young men were assembled in front of me with their legs spread apart, their hands neatly placed in back of their collared necks, and with their heads bowed despite their erect posture to best display their bodies. Amazingly, they were all about six feet tall, very muscular, and shared about the same body physiques. As requested, they were a variety of skin colors varying from pure white to a creamy brown to the yellow Asians to the pure black Africans. Their head hair varied from the long flowing stresses of almost pure white blondes to the short-cut kinky jet black curls of the Africans and everything in between. One up for inspection had bright red hair, a well-tanned ivory hide, and freckles despite the tan. All were at least 8" flaccid, thick in circumference, and neatly circumcised with large, but not freakish, balls. It was easy to view their organs since all had been completely body shaved. It was obvious Santos knew his stock well and what cages held what.

"If you don't like them smooth-skinned, master," Santos intoned, "you can always let it grow back. Five of these properties were covered in hair when we first got them. But we always show our stock smooth-skinned so a purchaser can easily see what he's getting."

"No, I like them smooth-skinned anyway," I replied, "so they'll need to stay that way."

"They're trained to keep themselves fully body shaved, Master, if that's what you want," Santos said assuringly. "Would you like to see them hard, Master?"

"Yes, just to be sure," I replied. Santos grabbed the first slave in the line, the aforementioned redhead, and began pumping his shaft vigorously. In less than 30 seconds, the slave was rock hard with a drop of pre-cum on the tip of his penis.

"That was fast," I exclaimed.

"Yes, master. They're not allowed any sexual outlets once they leave training so they respond well to the buyers' inspections. This boy here probably hasn't shot in at least a week or so - I think it's been that long since a buyer examined him rather thoroughly at that time."

"You mean he milked him then?" I asked.

"Yes, master. Most potential buyers want to see what their output looks like, both in terms of quantity as well as quality," Santos replied as if he were displaying a diary cow. "May I suggest, sir, that we feel it's a good idea before actually buying a boy. We want to make sure you know what you're getting, Master. These slaves are trained to expect nothing less of any buyer, master, and actually look forward to it, knowing this may be their only chance to discharge before another buyer shows up Lord knows when. Would you like me to stroke him to full eruption or would you prefer to do that yourself, Master? We usually catch the output in one of these little paper cups so you can see the total output plus have it handy to taste if you want."

"Not now, Santos. I'm not sure I want a red head in my team."

The slave under discussion tried to hide his disappointment in not being allowed to alleviate his need as well as his rejection of being bought. He knew he might sit in his cage for weeks before another buyer came along who was specifically looking for someone with his coloring and in the interim, without any relief, he knew he would be perpetually hard, dripping constantly, and almost obsessed thinking about alleviation of his sexual needs, especially in full view of all these other beautiful bodies being stroked, fondled and milked all around him. He bit his lip to keep from crying, but never broke his "display" stance knowing Santos' whip was ever ready and Santos loved to have an excuse to use it.

Santos quickly moved to the next slave and started stroking the huge semi-erect tool of the very handsome mulatto attached to the large organ. "Shall I bring him to fruition, Master?" Santos asked as his hand firmly wrapped around the organ and pumped away.

"Yes, he's looks like something I might want," I replied as I walked in back of the beautiful slave being milked and admired his tightly clenched ass, his muscular back and thighs, and his massive shoulders.

Within one minute, gob after gob of thick stringy cum was flowing in eruption after eruption into the paper cup until it was almost full and the slave was obviously spent, gasping for air as he struggled to maintain his equilibrium and perfect "display" posture. The orgasm had left his skin shiny with a light coating of sweat and his eyes slightly glazed.

Santos handed me the full cup. I sniffed the hot offering, sipped a little to appreciate its fresh, clean but salty taste, and ran a little between my fingers to see how thick it was. The cum was still steaming warm and had such a pleasant after-taste, I decided to quaff down the whole cup in one big swallow. It was creamy and thick and I savored it a while before sending it on its way down my gullet.

"Delicious, Santos. I'm surprised you aren't selling him as a milk stud."

"We would if that's what a buyer wanted," Santos laughed. "But I think you'll find most of these slaves can produce just as well as this mulatto boy. Keeping them caged does wonder for their output," Santos said with a professional tone.

"Where did Guiliono Imports get this boy?" I asked.

"I'm not sure, Master, but it would be in his provenance book on the stand here, quickly handing me the correct volume catalogued by cage number.

I opened the book and read.

"Male, age 19, 6.0 tall, 210 pounds. 8" flaccid, 11" erect. 4" penis circumference flaccid or erect. Purchased in Istanbul from our agent there 13 months ago who had obtained him from Istanbul prison authorities. Son of an Istanbul dock prostitute, this boy, according to the mother, is the product of her mating with an American black sailor, one of her steady customers at that time. Legal history starts at age 12 with purse snatching and other tourists annoyances, prostitution starting at age 14 in a brothel near the docks where his mother also worked, soliciting in gay bars and coffee hours throughout the city; and grand theft when he was 15. Placed in Istanbul prison following court sentencing for 10 years. Prison life characterized by prostitution to older prisoners for small favors, and ready adjustment to prison rules. No family known, so Director of Prisons sold him to agent along with his death certificate, which claimed he had been killed by older prisoners in a fight over his sexual favors. Took to slavery well once properly caged and food and water intake was totally controlled. Training proceeded without any troubles and fairly quickly. Slave himself states he is happier and more satisfied than at any time in his life and fully understands his only asset is his handsome body and that his body is the sole property of whoever buys him... Should adjust well to new owner, regardless of demands. No diseases, good health record to date. Purchase price: $350,000."

"I'll take him," I stated, closing the folder.

"Without fucking him first?" Santos said in some astonishment.

"I can't fuck them all, Santos," I explained with a smile.

"You want me to fuck him for your examination?" Santos countered.

"Takes too much time, although I may have you do that later if time allows."

"At least let the slave suck you, master," Santos almost pleaded. "He's very well trained in that area."

"I've no doubt that he is, Santos, but not now. We have a lot of others to pick out while we're here."

"Yes, master," Santos said, obviously thinking I was being a little hasty in my selection of stock. "But most buyers try a slave out thoroughly before buying them, master," Santos almost pleaded.

"Not this one, Santos - not when I'm got a whole team to buy up."

"Yes, master," Santos said resignedly as he moved to the next slave lined up before us, thinking of the weeks and weeks of training a slave received to handle being fucked thoroughly as part of any sales inspection.

———————

"Ah, a pure black," I said as I ran my hand quickly over the swelling pectorals of the next slave in line. I than reached down and tightly squeezed his balls, testing for reaction. He smiled and thrust his pelvis further into my hand.

"Cooperative," I commented as the black's penis swelled to full erection in seconds.

"Yes, master," Santos said. "Guiliano Imports got him with 19 others about a year ago from the Persian Gulf. "But I've taught him enough English to obey most commands," Santos said proudly as he sorted through the files until he found the one for this slave and handed it to me.

"Male, estimated age of 21, 6' 0" feet tall' 225 pounds. Penis 12" erect, 8" flaccid with 5" circumference fully erect, 4" flaccid. Bought in lot of 19 from Saudi Arabian prince who had received him as a gift from his grandfather when the slave was 18 and who served his owner as a personal body servant and bed buck. Owner died in unfortunate automobile accident and all of his slave stock (19) was sold to our Persian Gulf agent in that owner's family was currently overstocked with slaves themselves. Slaves from this lot are relatively unique in that all of them are products of the grandfather's selective slave breeding program which furnishes most of the royal household's current slave needs. This program stresses rigid adherence to breeding only the best stock while retaining pure blood lines. Therefore, this slave is a pure Mandingo black, being bred from full-blooded Mandingo slaves owned by the royal family for generations. Trained at the breeding program for full slave compliance, then specifically trained to serve as a competent bed buck and personal servant before being gifted to his grandson who used him in that capacity with a high degree of satisfaction according to our reports. Took to training in our facilities with little difficulty other than initial loneliness due to inability to communicate with anyone other than other slaves in his purchase lot. As a bred slave, he has no concept of

personal choice or individual freedom and is well adjusted to slave status and duties, readily performing any task asked of him. No diseases with excellent health. Purchase price: $360,000."

"Shall I milk him now," Santos asked, reaching for a paper cup, "or would you prefer to fuck him or have him suck you off first."

"I'll milk him," I said, taking the paper cup from him and proceeding to pump the black's huge staff until, quickly, the paper cup was full to overflowing.

"Blacks seem to have prodigious outputs," Santos commented, looking down at the spilt semen on the floor. "He can lick that up while you're tasting his juice," motioning for the black to quickly get down on the floor and lick up his overflow.

I sampled a little of the frothy warm output and then handed the cup back to the black being examined, motioning for him to drink it down. He did in one eager gulp, smacking his large lips together in appreciation.

"Shucrum," the black said with lowered eyes as he carefully put the emptied cup back on the nearby table.

"That's 'thank-you' in Arabic," Santos explained as the black quickly resumed his display position, still with a full erection.

"He's still hard as a rock," I commented.

"We could milk him two or three more times before he'd lose that trait," Santos laughed. "Some blacks are that way - especially the pure-breds like this one. They're always ready to go, seems like - some of the rest of us envy them."

"I'll take him," I said.

"You want me to demonstrate his fucking and sucking skills, master?" Santos asked. "He's very talented in both areas."

"Not now, Santos. We've got to move on here."

"Yes, master," Santos replied, obviously disappointed.

The next five purchases consisted of another pure black, this one a 20-year-old from a market in Chad; a Chinese 21-year-old bought by Giliano Imports at a Hong Kong market; another 19-year-old mulatto somehow illegally 'purchased' from a Texas prison in the United States; a showy blonde 21-year-old from Australia beautifully tanned kidnapped by Guiliano's Aussie agents and trained by Guiliano Imports for over two years now; and a hugely muscular blond lad Guiliano Imports had picked up in the Ukraine. All five were priced slightly lower than the two I'd already purchased. All had displayed well, all were obviously very eager to be purchased, and all responded to Santos' milking with eagerness.

I was a little unsure of the Aussie slave since his training has taken so long and he'd obviously been forced into slavery from different circumstances than the others. I asked Santos to fuck him then and there which the overseer did with vigor, eager, I think, to show off his fucking skills to me when he was in the driver's seat. I shouldn't have been concerned. The training has obviously been totally successful. The Aussie took to the fucking with no resentment or resistance evident and openly displayed his eagerness to being fucked, churning his ass at every chance to heighten his user's pleasure.

As Santos withdrew after shooting a full load up the boy's ass, I asked him if the Aussie was naturally gay.

"I don't think so, Master," he laughed. "I bet we had to rape that boy 200 times before he learned to relax and enjoy it. But," he paused as the fucked slave quickly cleaned his shaft with his mouth, "he sure seems to appreciate a good fucking now, doesn't he?"

"That he does," I admitted as I felt the Aussie's prominent tits, now fully erect and, reaching with my other hand, stroked the slave's quivering erect prick.

"You like getting fucked now?" I asked the boy under examination in English.

"Yes, master," the Aussie said respectfully as he pushed his penis further into my hand. "Very much so."

"In that case, I'd like you and your overseer in my suite tonight," nodding to Santos to make sure he understood.

"We'll be there," Santos promptly answered, obviously pleased that at last I was going to test out one of my purchases and possibly use his body once again.

"Santos, I'm getting a little tired. We've got two more purchases to go, but I think I'll put those off until after breakfast tomorrow. I've seen about all the slaves up for inspection I can handle for one day, I think."

"Yes, master," Santos said understandingly. "If you'll just give me a minute to cage the stock back up and mark the cages of those already sold. It won't take me long, master." With that, he again grabbed his riding crop and began to usher the stock back to their small cages, but then paused.

"Do you want the Australian slave with you now, master, or do you want him sent to your room around bedtime?"

"Bedtime, with you with him," I smiled. "I wanted time to chat with the Russian agent who delivered some new stock after dinner."

With that, he quickly re-caged the stock and led me back to the main facility where dinner would be served shortly while I casually looked at some of the other caged stock available.

When Santos returned, he saw me peering into the cages nearest the door.

'If you see anything that interests you, just let me know and you can examine them tomorrow," he said. "You may see some stock outside your original specifications which you may want to purchase over and beyond your team requirements."

"You're quite the salesman, Santos," I laughed, "as well as a good overseer and we both know you're damn good in bed."

"Yes, master, but don't forget the seven languages I speak," he responded with a huge smile lighting up his face. "I can even scream in ecstasy in all seven languages if you so desire it to heighten the experience."

"No wonder Guiliano hangs on to you," I laughed back. "You're too good to let loose."

———————

The Russian agent proved as interesting as Aristo Mythos promised and, to Mythos's surprise, he spoke English well, so Santos serving as a translator wasn't needed. As the three men supped together, waited on by three extremely attractive house slaves, naked save for their heavy metal collars, the Russian explained where he had obtained the lot of slaves he had just delivered.

"Russia's a strange place these days," he started out. "The economic situation is desperate for many, and so a lot of boys without families hit the streets trying to supplement their meager incomes from the factories. When the factories close, they go into selling themselves full-time but soon find they need a "sponsor" or they get beaten up and aren't allowed any customers whatsoever, no matter what they look like. After the Mafia takes them over, it's just a matter of time until they end up in one of the Mafia's brothels where they put out on schedule or are quickly whipped into shape, let me tell you. After there is no resistance left in them and they do what they're told without questioning it anymore, the Mafia picks out the best looking among them to beef them out with a lot of forced exercises and good food, gets them immunized against all the major diseases, teaches them proper grooming techniques, and then starts to market them internationally. By this time they pretty well know there's no going back - the few that balk end up floating in the nearest river as an example to the others - and gradually accept the fact they're now just owned properties.

When they're first referred to as slaves instead of just boys, they're usually shocked, but eventually the reality of their situation sinks into them, especially since they're usually shackled most of the time now and are totally dependent on their 'masters' for their food and shelter. By the time it comes to market them abroad, they usually aren't too concerned when we cage them for shipment. Most of them feel their new life certainly won't be any worse than working the brothels day and night and might even be better. Slaves are that way, Mr. Parsimi. They always think the next sale will lead to a better life. I don't know why, but that's the way they think."

"How many stock do you obtain that way?" I asked.

"Oh, maybe 20 to 30 percent."

"Where do you get the others?"

"The old state-run orphanages are a big source. The supervisors there, left with no funds whatsoever since the collapse of the Soviets, simply sell off their inmates that have come of age and are fully developed. It's the only way they can raise any funds to take care of their youngest charges. The orphans don't have any say in it at all - one day they're orphans, the next day they're shackled, collared, and find themselves in an agent's holding cell in some warehouse somewhere. We agents typically sort them out and market the best looking, best hung ones to places like this, Guiliano Imports. The rest we sell out to third world countries looking for cheap labor where no questions are ever asked. It's quite a lucrative market either way. Even the ugly ones bring a good price if you can find the right labor market. Of course," the Russian agent smiled, "some of them take considerable training before we can market them with confidence."

Aristo Mythos laughed. "That's the understatement of the year. Some boys like that take up to 12 or 13 months before they're properly broken to slavery. When we buy boys like that, we always have to figure in the considerable training costs involved as well as feeding them all the time they're learning what being a slave is all about."

"Well, at least the Mafia brothel slaves are fairly easily trained," the Russian countered.

"That I admit," Mythos laughed again. "Four or five months of good rigid training for the world market and they're ready for even Guiliano Imports to market them."

"And your other sources?" I asked.

"Well, we buy up prisoners from the state-run prisons, but only those without any family and usually only those given death sentences or at least life imprisonment. The prisons are glad to get rid of them and what use to cost them in food and housing turns into a tidy profit. Of course, only the young and able are marketable, but that's the bulk of their new prisoners anyway. Those poor souls are glad to be sold - it sure beats the alternative - and accept their slavery easily enough it seems like. I imagine they're easy to train, aren't they, Aristo?"

"They're certainly the easiest of the Russian stock we get," Aristo said. "Slavery to them isn't any different than their prison life, they never had any freedom there anyway, and they were routinely fucked half to death while being incarcerated. So being sold off as a slave doesn't mean much of a life style change for them. The real problem we have is getting them back into good health and building up their physique to market standards. But getting them used to being bedded down, following the orders of others instantly, and all that - it's a piece of cake with these former prisoners. Of course we're only buying the best looking, heavy hung boys anyway, so they were probably used to be fucked at every opportunity while they were serving their time in those drab Russian prisons."

"What about those prisoners not very good looking?" I asked.

"There's a good market for them - anywhere cheap labor is wanted. You can't beat slave labor when it comes to cost. Even feeding them well, you still can pay back their cost in 5 to 8 years if you've got a good overseer who knows how to manage slaves and isn't timid when it comes to proper discipline," the Russian replied.

"Yes," Aristo Mythos added, "good management is essential with any slaves - whether they're good looking or not. And all slaves need to be kept in an environment of rigid discipline for their own good."

"Santos seems to be an excellent overseer," I commented. "I notice he always carries that little riding crop in his right hand and he's not afraid to use it at the slightest provocation."

"Santos is good," Aristo confirmed. "Being a slave for years now himself, he fully understands a slave is only happy and content when he knows what is expected of him and what the clear-cut boundaries of his existence are. Translated, that means Santos lets his boys know exactly what they're going to do with a happy smile on their face or get their ass whipped until they can't walk for a week and their food, water, and sex outlets cut until they can think of nothing else but their bodily needs. The judicial administration of pain, combined with rigid control of how a body can fulfill their natural needs to survive, is a great educator, Mr. Parsimi. Santos understands that - he's been through it all himself and he knows, once a slave accepts that fact, he can be happy and content in his new life. He certainly is as I'm sure you have noticed."

"Yes," I smiled. "I've going to enjoy him and a new Australian slave I bought in my bed tonight."

"Once wasn't enough, huh, Mr. Parsimi," Mythos smiled. "It seldom is with Santos, as I can vouch for myself."

"I feel cheated," the Russian laughed. "We dealers are never allowed to use Guiliano's own stock, so I'm always stuck with the Russian stock I bring in. But I'm not complaining. The last batch worked out very well and I've got a couple of those prison boys shackled to my bed as we speak awaiting my evening's pleasure."

"Fucked to death by the time we take title on them," Mythos chuckled.

"No, just starting their serious training," the Russian laughed in return.

"And you, Mr. Parsimi, are looking for some new slave stock here?" the Russian asked.

"Yes, eight to be exact. I'm buying them as litter bearers among other things," I replied.

"Litter bearers? They still use those contraptions in your country?" the Russian looked startled.

"No, but I want one on my estate just for the fun of it. It's a big ornate thing with lots of room and will take eight big and sturdy slaves to make it work right. Should be lots of fun to show my friends, and, of course, I'll use those big handsome studs in a lot of other ways too," I explained.

"A literal harem," the Russian said enviously.

"That's the plan," I replied.

"A final coffee for anyone?" Mythos asked. When we nodded in the negative, he invited us to look over our waiters who, like everyone else on the island, was for sale. "Perhaps you'd like to have them suck you off as an after-dinner treat?" he invited.

We looked them over as they stood next to us in full display position with their semi-erect organs thrust out for our convenience in handling them. One was a handsome young black boy, another a striking Asian man of about 25 with magnificent musculature, and the third was a very well equipped blond boy of about 20 who Mythos said was from Argentina. But both the Russian and I declined further use of them in that both of us wanted to save our output for the slaves that awaited us in our guest suites.

"Oh, very well," Mythos said as he continued stroking the muscular Asian slave nearest him. "I'll just bed them down myself if you don't mind."

We all laughed as Mythos led the three slaves in attendance back to his quarters by their neck leashes and the Russian and I headed back to our own guest rooms.

That night, the Australian proved he was indeed a rare find and that he was completely and thoroughly trained in all aspects of what a slave was expected to do for his master these days. His sucking skills were excellent and his ass was well trained to deliver a most satisfying fuck. The Aussie seemed to enjoy whatever demands were placed upon him and thanked me profusely for using him each time I did. Santos was even better than in the boat coming over and, since we had plenty of time, I fucked him three times before we all went to sleep.

At breakfast the next morning, the Russian looked exhausted, but well satisfied, reporting he hated to part with the Russian slaves he had bedded down last night. Mythos said the same about the three waiters he had taken to his quarters, but muttered something about business being business and all slaves here were just market commodities and there were plenty more from wherever those slaves came from.

I soon joined Santos once again for the final selections. He again had the stock he'd originally selected and which I hadn't already bought exercised, cleaned up, and back in the display area. He reminded me that if I wanted a good variety, it might be good to look at a Latino and a Polynesian and, when I nodded my ascent, quickly led me to two he thought might do.

Both were exactly the same height and weight of the stock I'd already purchased, were just as well built and heavily hung as the others, and certainly looked equal to the task of hefting the heavy litter rather easily. Both were very good looking with well chiseled muscular definition on very handsome bodies and both had unusually beautiful facial features. The Latino was a rich dark brown with almost feline facial features with his green eyes, dark eyebrows and heavy eyelashes. The Polynesian was a much lighter brown with a smooth milky complexion, blue eyes also heavily lashed, and magnificent pectoral development topped with large brown nipples. Both were at least 8" flaccid which quickly grew once I started handling them.

"They're well trained, master," Santos said. "Would you like to try them out?"

"I don't have the strength after being with you all night, and I doubt if you do either," I laughed.

"Well, I'll milk them first," Santos said as he reached for the paper cup, "unless, of course, you want to, master."

"Oh, go ahead," I said as I began to seriously look over their bodies front and back.

Within a minute, Santos had a full discharge out of the Latino which, in six successive spurts, quickly filled the cup almost to the top while the Latino bucked and heaved some in the throe of his orgasm trying to control his verbal moans as he emptied his balls. Santos quickly moved to the Polynesian and within no longer a time, had that slave spurting his juices out into a fresh cup, breaking out into a full sex sweat as he did so which covered his body with a nice sheen. Both slaves were a good 12" in full erection, but quickly shrank back to 8" when they had completed their milking although their 5" circumference remained the same.

I drank down both cups of hot cum in that it was one of my favorite breakfast treats and these slaves' output was particularly fresh and tasty. It might be a good idea to milk all eight studs I was buying every morning, I thought, in that it would give me a good fresh supply each and every day and wouldn't hurt the stock one iota. I mentioned this idea to Santos who thought it was an excellent plan and assured me the slaves would like nothing better, reminding me that the milking would probably be their only chance to alleviate their own needs. I hadn't thought of that, but could see where the slaves would appreciate such an opportunity to have a satisfying orgasms even if on schedule every day, especially if there were no other opportunities afforded them.

"They'll be forever grateful," Santos assured me, "and love their master all the more for it. Look at that grateful look in their eyes right now," he added and sure enough, the slave's eyes reflected their intense gratitude at finally being allowed to shoot off themselves and relieve the chronic aching of their overfilled balls.

"I guess I should see if they fuck OK," I murmured as I finished the last of my breakfast treat. "Would you mind fucking them for me, Santos, of should we just have them fuck each other?"

"I'll be delighted to fuck them, master," Santos said, "but if they fuck each other, you could judge how well they take a fucking as well as how well they can fuck on command, master."

"Good idea, Santos," I replied.

Without further ado, Santos ordered the Latino on all fours and the Polynesian to mount him for a deep fucking. I was surprised the Polynesian had the strength to do so after just being milked and mentioned it to Santos.

"They're trained to last through three or four orgasms if that's what their master wants," Santos explained. "It will be no problem."

And indeed it wasn't. The Polynesian pumped long and deep into the Latino's ass while I studied the Latino's face as he handled the huge intrusion up his rear. At first the Latino bucked and wiggled a bit to better accommodate the large shaft entering him, but soon settled down to the steady rhythm of the pounding with only a constant low moan of ecstasy issuing from him as his own organ swelled and started dripping heavily as he reacted to being fucked so vigorously. The look of ecstasy on his face revealed he'd obviously learned to enjoy this aspect of his slavery and he now welcomed his own whoredom.

"Did he always enjoy it like this?" I asked Santos.

"Hardly," Santos snickered. "He fought being fucked a lot more than most - Latinos are that way - they come in here thinking you're not a man unless you're doing the fucking. But after a while, you realize you're not raping them anymore - they relax and begin to enjoy it. By the time they're through training, they crave it as you can see for yourself with this slave here. He's a natural whore and just didn't know it," Santos laughed. "Slavery has revealed his true self just like it did with me."

When I indicated I'd seen enough, even though the Polynesian hadn't shot into the boy's butt yet, Santos had them trade places, but this time with the Polynesian on his back with his legs lifted as the Latino mounted him from the front and entered him in one huge stroke, the Polynesian's slimy prick sliding between the two bodies. The Polynesian was a little nosier in taking a fuck, groaning as the Latino's large shaft quickly entered him, squirming around until his rectum stretched, and then moaning with each new thrust into him as his arms reached around and started scratching the back and rump of the Latino drilling into him.

"Stop that scratching, you whore," Santos said as his riding crop nipped at the sides of the Polynesian's torso. "You know better than that."

"Yes sir. Sorry, sir," the Polynesian moaned as his scratching turned instantly into gently caressing his fellow slave's back and he pressed his hole even further onto the prick well within him.

"Well, they both seem trained in that department well enough," I said as I motioned the demonstration could stop.

Santos ordered both slaves back to a full display position, their erect pricks now dripping with each other's ass juices. "They're trained not to just accept a good fucking, but to actually enjoy it," Santos said with some satisfaction since he had been in charge of their training.

"Yes, it certainly seemed that way," I conceded. "But a slave's lot is to do what he is told whether he enjoys it or not," I cautioned.

"Certainly, master," Santos quickly replied, "but we have found that if a slave enjoys it too, he never loses his initial training in the area."

"You've got a point there. We can't always have a slave in training, now can we?" I laughed. "Santos, I'll take these two you picked out to complete my litter team."

"Yes, master. Would you like to see some other stock while you're here?" Santos said. "We have some other interesting stock caged right here, and then there are well over a thousand in our training facilities, not counting the new Russians brought in yesterday."

"Always the salesman, aren't you, Santos? The only time you haven't been hustling stock was when I was fucking you. That seems to settle you down at least temporarily," I laughed.

"Sorry if I was too forward, master," Santos said sincerely. "Perhaps instead you would like to fuck me again?"

"Not now. Maybe on the boat going back to Delos. I need to get back to Italy to stay on schedule. I take it you can handle getting the eight slaves shipped to my estate in a reasonable time?"

"Master Mythos will go over those details with you, Master, along with the payment procedures. Meanwhile, Master, I will be cleaning and preparing the stock for shipment in their cages in that we ship sold stock out fairly quickly, Master - just as soon as your payment clears the bank."

"How are they shipped?"

"On one of our own small vessels. They look like fishing boats on the outside, but inside, they're fitted out for quick secure shipment of slaves to their new homes. When they get to port, the slaves are drugged, their cages are crated up so no one can see their contents and they are transported to a closed truck which will deliver them right to your estate's slave quarters, master. The drug we use will wear off about the time you uncrate them on delivery at your estate so they'll be frisky and ready to use the minute they arrive and are fed and watered. Although we completely clean them with four successive enemas before shipment and don't feed them from this moment on, they still may need a good cleaning before you put them to use. But, master, in your case, I doubt it. It should only take eight or nine hours to reach the port nearest your estate in our high speed boats and another couple of hours by truck. Most stock don't mess themselves until they're caged for 24 hours or longer if they're cleaned out properly to start with."

"Santos, you're a wonder," I exclaimed. "If Guiliano ever decides to sell you, tell them to notify me first. I'll outbid them all to get you as my chief overseer."

"Thank you, master, and what a pleasure it would be to serve as your property. I shall be sure to tell my owners that if they decide to sell me."

With that, Santos led the two slaves I had just bought back to their cages before starting shipping preparations for the whole batch.

Meanwhile, I met with Mythos who quickly tallied up the purchases, prepared all the sales papers and certificates of ownership, and arranged for me to electronically transfer the necessary funds to the Guiliano account in Switzerland. When that cleared within minutes, he carefully put all the slave's provenance and health records, along with their certificates of ownership and bills of sale and the keys to their shipping cages into a large leather portfolio.

"Anything else you'll like to see while you're here?" Aristo asked.

"Well, I do have about three hours before my plane is scheduled to arrive. Would it be possible to see some of your training facilities?"

"Of course, Mr. Parsimi. I can at least give you some idea of how we handle fresh stock just being shipped in, some boys about half way through their training, and boys in the final stages right before we put them up for sale. We ought to be able to get that done in a couple of hours or so. Just follow me," he said graciously as he led me out the door for about a four-block walk to a huge building surrounded by electrified fence, double door entrances, and other features of most any maximum-security prison. There didn't seem to be any windows whatsoever and the doors were solid metal so no one could see in or out.

The guards quickly opened the doors for us and, once inside, it was bright and airy - huge skylights, high above the area below and heavily grated with iron bars, filled most of the roof and could be opened to allow fresh breezes to enter - which they were at the moment. The walls were plain cement block but most were covered with small individual cages, stacked five high with walkways outside each of the levels for easy access. Trainers were much in evidence, identifiable by their leather body harnesses and the numerous whips and electrical prods fastened to their harness for ready access. Most carried a 6' whip in their right hand which seemed to be made of some synthetic material resembling cowhide and which branched out into 12 separate lashes. Other than that, they looked like most of the others in the building: naked, collared, branded on their right pectoral with Guiliano's own brand, and some tit-ringed and genitally banded.

"The best trainers are slaves themselves," Aristo explained as he saw me staring at them. "It seems you know how to train a lot better if you've been through it yourself. Using non-slaves as trainers works, but it's just not as good. Non-slaves are either too hard on the new stock or too lenient, whereas slave trainers seem to know exactly how far to push a slave on any given day without having them beat to death or getting off too easy for effective slave training."

"Interesting," I replied as I watched one of the trainers order one of his charges down over a sawhorse for shackling, and, when the slave didn't move quickly enough for him, lashed out with his whip until the slave was screaming in agony, his back a mass of ugly red and purple bruises, almost diving down over the sawhorse to get in the commanded position.

"These slaves here are mid-way through their training as you can probably judge from all those whip marks on them everywhere a whip can reach. The new Mylar whips we're using are a godsend - they hurt worse than any whip we've ever used and bruise a boy up for a lasting impression but they rarely lacerate the skin. Before we started using them, most of our slaves' bodies were pretty well scarred up by the time they finished training and there used to be blood all over the floor in here. Now training goes somewhat faster and we can sell a finished product with very few permanent scars on their pretty bodies."

By that time, the slave just disciplined was draped over the sawhorse being vigorously fucked by his trainer's exceptionally large penis. The trainee made no sign of resistance; instead he was busily churning his ass to heighten his user's experience and was moaning softly as his body was being used. His own organs were rapidly swelling in response to being fucked - a sure sign he was responding appropriately for a slave.

"Won't be too long until he's a full-fledged whore," Aristo Mythos laughed as he watched the slave's organs beginning to drip profusely in the excitement of being fucked. Once they reach that stage and are able to get similarly excited at being ordered to suck someone off, they're almost ready to market successfully."

All around me, slaves were being fucked, were sucking their trainers, were having huge dildos driven up their asschutes, or were standing complacently while their trainers played with their tits, their balls, or fondled other parts of their bodies.

"These slaves are through the basic slave response training - you know, learning to kneel, position, get on all fours, and wait at ease with their heads and eyes lowered. And by this time they generally respond to any and all commands without question or any hesitancy. What we're doing now it shaping them into responding immediately, always demonstrating subservience and humility, and learning thoroughly their body is for their new owner's pleasure no matter what he or she may want. They know they're a slave long before they get to this stage of training - now we're working on making them a slave of some value. Before the trainers are finished with them in here, they'll take considerable pride in doing what's asked of them to the very best of their abilities. This stage generally takes three or four months for most of the stock."

"How long for the initial slave training?" I asked.

"A little longer if slavery's new to them. Usually about five to eight months with extremes both ways. If we get ahold of a person who was a slave before, it doesn't take much time at all of course. Same's true if they were a lifer prisoner somewhere - life as a slave isn't much different than their life before so they adjust quickly. But some, generally middle-class spoiled kids who are kidnapped or debtors sold to us by the Mafia can take up to a year before they're properly broken to slavery. But they all break at some point or another, believe you me," Aristo laughed.

"How do you know they actually accepted their new status?" I asked.

"I'll show you," Aristo replied as he led me to another whole area of the huge building. "This is where we train brand new stock. Look, over there are those Russian boys that were just delivered yesterday. They look scared to death, are embarrassed at being displayed without a stitch of clothing on them, and are still trying to hide their genitals. That's the way new stock generally behaves. But you'll be amazed how quickly they adjust to being nude all the time, especially when everyone else is in the same condition, and a good solid whippings every day lets them know that no nonsense in cooperating with us will be tolerated. It's important to beat them soundly at first - until they think they're going to die from being beaten work's best. Then they get no water and no food until they do something we want they wouldn't dream of doing in their old life - like standing on full display with their hands in back of their necks while we run our hands all over their bodies. We don't allow any sexual outlets with new stock, so after a while they're constantly horny which only helps the training. Hell, we don't even allow them to shit or piss without getting our permission. Any hint of resistance to any of this gives us a good excuse to beat them senseless with our Mylar whips, shock them at the slightest provocation with these electric prods or withhold their food and water until they think they might die. Sounds harsh, but it really works, especially if you start right in on them the minute they arrive. Those Russians, for example, will not get any food or water for at least 48 hours no matter how well they behave simply so they learn whose in control of their lives now, they won't be allowed to jerk themselves off, and they'll be beaten several times even if they haven't done anything wrong - the theory is they're beaten just because they're now slaves and slaves need to be beaten for their own good. By nightfall, they will have been forcibly fucked three or four times shackled to those sawhorses over there and before the week is out, they will have been forced to suck their trainers off three or four times every day. Our trainers claim constant fuckings, combined with a heavy whip, are what acclimates a slave best. I don't know - seems to me food, water, and sex deprivation would have a big hand in it. Well, at any rate, buckle under they do. And, you know, Mr. Parsimi, once a slave buckles under he pretty well stays that way the rest of his life. Good training seems to be a lifelong proposition - kind of like learning to ride a bike - you never forget it."

"When do they acquire those beautiful physiques I saw on every single slave you had up for sale?" I asked.

"We work on that from day one. Those Russians over there, for example, will be put into a heavy exercise routine for four hours starting today under the whip and prods where they'll give it everything they've got or get beaten half to death. That four-hour routine stays with every slave here right up to the time they're sold and shipped out. Nobody's going to pay much for a slave not in top condition these days, but by the time they reach the marketing stage, the slaves have learned to enjoy all those exercises and have learned to take considerable pride in their beautiful bodies.'

"Why would they take pride?" I asked, rather innocently.

"Their body is all they've got anymore, even if it does belong to someone else now. You've got to have pride in something and they know they've got splendid bodies now. But most of them also take pride in being a good slave, fucking well, pleasing their owner, and all the rest of it before they're marketed. It's how a slave carves out a life for himself. How valued am I? How much to people admire my body? Is my master or mistress pleased with me? Do other slaves look up to me? Would other masters like to owe me? It's all a slave has to define themselves. Despite the fact they are just slaves, they are still human, despite the fact we often just view them as livestock."

"You should look at our correctional center," Aristo Mythos said as he led me to another area.

Here the walls were covered with embedded shackles, leg irons were fastened to the cement floor, stretch racks and whipping posts were everywhere, and on numerous tables and stands were huge assortments of various types of whips, huge dildos, mouth gags, jaw restraints, mouth bits, butt plugs, thrashing rods, wicked looking whipping canes, catheters and even a few hot branding irons smoldering in one corner. In yet another corner were the facilities to fit various types of slave collars, everything from the simple hinged metal collars used in training with a padlock to the thick welded type found on most slaves sold off, tit rings of all types and description, genital bands of every material and thickness, wrist, arm, and ankle bands, along with all sorts of shackles, leg irons, etc. A long row of benches equipped with various sized dildos embedded in the bottom bench had chains cleverly attached so that slaves could be impaled on the dildos and then chained so they had no choice but to remain seated with the enormous dildo stretching their insides. Not one control device had been overlooked, it seemed.

"Well equipped," was all I could say.

"Yes," Aristo agreed. "And well used. Almost every slave in training visits this room frequently for some infraction or another no matter how hard they try. And, of course, we can fit out slaves being sold to their new owner's specifications. It won't be long until those eight you bought will be back here being fitted with the tit rings and genital bands you ordered along with their new welded collars to match.

As we talked, several slaves, passed out from the pain of their discipline, were being removed from their shackles on the wall and dragged back to their cages while others were being chained to the whipping post. Within minutes, as the whipping commenced, the place was filled with the slave's screams of anguish that seemed to reflect the fact they had no way of escaping their master's discipline, no matter what form it took. Still others were shackled by their arms and knees to a nearby table while huge dildos were forced up their backsides as the slaves begged and pleaded for mercy, but none was forthcoming from the trainers. Others were impaled with butt plugs, chained tight to the bench holding the plugs, so that their own body weight forced the plugs further and further into them.

"What trouble did these slaves get themselves into?" I asked, looking at both the slaves on the whipping post and the slaves locked to the table on their hands and wide-spread knees with their ass forced open as wide as it would go as giant dildos were being forced up them.

"Nothing outside the routine, probably," Mythos answered. "Otherwise, they would be getting some memorable shocks where it really hurts," he laughed. "They probably balked doing something quickly enough after being ordered to do so, or they may have given a resentful look to one of the trainers or they may have forgotten to have thanked their trainers for correcting them with just a normal whipping. We don't tolerate such nonsense around here A judicious amount of pain administered at just the right moment makes a lasting impression on a slave and helps them adjust to the realities of their lives more quickly."

"Do you expect these slaves to thank the trainers after they been disciplined to this extent?" I asked.

"If they're still conscious, of course, Mr. Parsimi. A slave has to learn he should always be grateful when a master corrects him. Such correctional discipline is what makes him become a better slave. Most slaves figure that out eventually."

"Of course," I answered. "Only makes sense."

"Those slaves you bought are fully trained to thank you for your discipline. If you are negligent in that area, they're trained to remind you of it. They've been taught that's the only way they can be of utmost satisfaction to you."

"Good," I responded. "That way I won't feel guilty when they're screaming in pain."

"Just the opposite, Mr. Parsimi. You should feel proud you're being a good master - one they are trained to relate to."

At that moment, the eight slaves I had purchased were ushered in by Santos wielding his whip over their backs to keep them in exact line and positioned where he wanted them. He greeted the two of us heartedly with a quick wave of his hand as he shackled each of my new slaves to a separate "fitting" table where they would be unable to move a muscle. The "fitter" soon started in on the first slave I'd purchased, the Turk, removing his old training collar and replacing it with a new shiny metal one, welded it on with a great shower of sparks. He then quickly fitted the genital band, making sure it was good and tight before welding it shut, again with a great display of sparks.

"Doesn't that welding gun burn them?" I asked.

"Not directly, but the collars and bands heat up quite a bit in the welding and the hot metal often burns the slaves a little but it heals fast enough - nothing like the branding they've all endured," he scoffed. "Those surface burns hurt like hell, but they heal up fine in a few days. We put an antiseptic cream on the burns and will send some for you to use if you want in their shipping crates which you should apply for two or three days after you get them."

Lastly, the fitter quickly pierced each of the slave's nipples, inserted the ordered rings, and welded them shut - this time with the slave screaming in pain rather than just groaning and gritting their teeth like they did when the tight collars and ever tighter genital bands were installed. Those being fitted had every muscle in their body showing the strain from their tit-piercing and the quick ring insertion through the sensitive piercing. Each slave was left gasping for air in a sea of tears by the time the rings were installed, blood running down their chests from the piercings.

"Nothing like tit-rings and genital bands to remind a slave of just what he is," Aristo remarked. "You'll be happy you're fitting them out this way. They'll appreciate it in the long haul. It's a constant reminder their body is your property. Even now, they're already thinking all this is being done to them at the mere whim of a powerful master who now controls them and their body in all ways. It's a powerful lesson. I wish all slave owners had the sense to fit slaves out this way. They would have happier, more content slaves in the long haul."

"Santos claimed it was as effective as branding," I reflected.

"Well, he should know," Aristo chuckled. "He's been fitted out with rings and bands since we first acquired him."

"How long for their tits to heal up?" I asked.

"The bleeding will stop within the hour probably, but those tits are going to be mighty sore and susceptible to infection for up to two weeks for most slaves. We'll lavish their tits with antiseptic cream as soon as they stop bleeding and tape the rings to their chest so they don't swing around and start the bleeding again. I'd suggest you spread that cream on them for a good 10 days and keep their rings taped tight to their chest. After that, they'll be fine and those rings will swing around on their tits like they've always been there. Makes a handy thing to leash them by once they're completely healed," Aristo commented. "A boy leashed by his tits doesn't give his owner one drop of trouble. We send out plenty of strapping tape and antibiotic cream with each delivery that's had its tit's ringed so you won't need to buy anything extra. Other than that, no special considerations are needed. You can fuck them the moment you get them - just remember not to play with their tits while you're doing it for the first couple of weeks. After that, those tits are all yours and, after a boy's ringed, they just grow and grow until there's something substantial to play with," he winked. "You'll be happy you had it done. Over time, your slave boys will learn to appreciate them too."

"Sounds good," was all I could think of saying, having no expertise in the area myself.

"Santos keeps slaves on a strict schedule," Aristo Mythos laughed. "He'll have them in their shipment cages before we can get you back to Delos. But we still have a little time for you to visit the last stage of training here."

This area was close to the shipping docks, where stock was first bought in and, a good many months later, shipped out to new owners.

Slaves in this area were unshackled, sported perpetual semi-erections, and seemed to possess a calm demeanor as they responded to their trainer's commands. All had a pleasant smile on their face and seemed eager to please, not out of fear, but out of pride. Most of their naked bodies were healing up nicely from the numerous "corrections" they had received in their prior training - none showed open lacerations and most had only a few purple, green, and yellow bruises marking their bodies as remembrances of past lessons. It was obvious their bodies would be without blemish by the time they were marketed. And what bodies they were after months and months of forced exercise and weight-lifting to obtain clear definition. Magnificent to a man, they almost strutted in pride of their bodies, showing them off at every opportunity to each other, to their trainers, and certainly to us as visitors. Most thrust their pelvises out when they saw us, again proud to display their large genitals, now almost constantly erect. All had an inviting smile on their face as they went about their duties of sucking each other off, getting fucked, fucking, fondling another's body, or standing quietly as they were milked - all under the careful direction of their trainers.

"We're a long way from those Russian boys trying to hide their genitals," I laughed.

"Yes," Aristo laughed with me. "But those Russian boys will be strutting their stuff just like these boys here in a few months."

"I don't doubt it - not after what I've seen here this morning. Unfortunately, I'll need to get started back, interesting as this place is," I replied.

"Of course, Mr. Parsimi." With that, we left this last segment of the training center and Aristo Mythos led me back to the main facility's front door.

———————

"Very pleasant doing business with you, Mr. Parsimi. If you have any problems with the shipment or with the slaves once you have them toting that big litter of yours around the estate, just let me know. Guiliano takes pride in their products and will stand in back of our training procedures. Occasionally, we have to bring a boy back for retraining, but not too often. Still, if you encounter any problems at all in any area, just give me a call and we'll have the slave back here for a serious round of retraining or give you a new one of equal value instead. Santos assures me you have made some excellent choices among our stock." With that he gave me his card and led me to the front door where Santos, stark naked as usual, was awaiting me for the return trip to Delos.

"Santos will see you to your plane. Bon voyage, Mr. Parsimi, and remember to take advantage of Santos on the way back as a parting remembrance."

That's exactly what I did the minute the boat was on autopilot and this time it was even better than the previous night. I fucked him until it was time to dock whereupon he again donned his clothing, docked the boat, greeted his friends on the piers, and got the BMW for the short trip to the airstrip.

"Want to use me again before the plane, Master?" Santos said with a big smile. "I can always pull over in a grove of trees if you want."

"Thanks but no thanks, Santos. Don't you ever wear out?"

"No master," he chuckled. "I love whoring even better than lording it over those slaveboys back on the island."

"I'm beginning to believe it. But I will say, Santos, you're damn good at both from what I've seen."

"Thank you, master, and I won't forget your offer to buy me if the opportunity arises," he smiled.

With that, we were at the waiting airplane and Santos quickly helped me in and placed my overnight case in the luggage compartment of the chartered plane.

The pilot promptly started the engines and took off. I wondered if I would ever see the fabulous Santos again?

―――――――――

Within 13 hours of my own arrival at the estate, a large truck was at the front gate asking for clearance stating they had an express shipment from Guiliano Imports. After I told them the route to take to the delivery area, I quickly pushed the button to open the electric gates and hurried out to supervise the unloading. My trusted steward was right behind me and, I knew, would handle all of the details once the crates were unloaded and the truck was long on its way back to the port.

"There's eight of these crates, sir, and they must weight over 300 pounds each. We'll need to use the power lift gate to get them off the truck," the burly driver stated almost apologetically nodding to his assistant to start shoving the first crate back to the power lift. Between the two of them, they had all eight crates on the ground in back of my estate within ten minutes.

"What's in those crates, anyway?" the assistant asked. "They're sure heavy. Smells like animals or something."

"Some art work from Greece," I explained. "Very delicate. That's why I had it shipped special handling and express. I suppose that odor you thought you smelled is due to the straw they often pack the art in. I knew you guys always take real good care when its marked special handling and I thought the express charges were worth it so they didn't get lost in some warehouse somewhere," I explained jovially, handing each of them a sizable tip.

"Thanks, sir," both of the truck drivers exclaimed, obviously pleased when they saw the tip was indeed generous. "Hope you find that stuff in good shape. We tried to get it here as quick as we could."

"I'm sure it is - thanks to you," I replied as I quickly signed the receipts they had handed me, signifying I had received the crates at such and such a time.

"If you want, sir, for a little extra, we could stick around and uncrate the stuff for you," the head driver ventured. "We made such good time up here we would stick around 30 more minutes or so and still make it back in time so as not to get the boss on our back."

"No thanks," I replied. This stuff is better left crated just like it is until I can get around to dealing with it now that you're got it here safe and sound. I don't have time to fiddle with it right now. But thank's anyway. I appreciate the offer."

The truckers were so happy with their generous tip they didn't try to hustle the estate's owner any more and quickly drove the truck out the exit, jabbering to each other the whole way about their good fortune in delivering something, at last, to a person who knew enough to tip a driver who'd done a good job.

As soon as the front gate was again secure, my steward immediately took a crow bar and begin prying the boards lose from the cages underneath. Quickly revealed were eight sturdy metal cages lined with straw, each with a magnificent body stuffed into it just now beginning to move just a little.

"Just like they said, Sergei," I said to my steward of many years, a Polish slave I had bought over 10 years ago from a underground dealer peddling his stock in Italy at the time, "the drug is just now beginning to wear off. If we wait a few minutes, they can walk of their own steam back to the slave quarters where you can get them cleaned up, fed, and watered. Then you can have them move their cages back into the storage room - we may need them if we ever sell them!"

"Yes, master. Should I give them a series of enemas when I'm cleaning them, master?" Sergei asked pointedly.

"Might as well, Sergei. It'll get them used to the routine and I really don't know which of them I may want to use yet today."

"Yes, master," the steward replied with lowered eyes. "The new stock is certainly first quality, master, if I may say so. I don't think I've ever seen eight prettier and better built bodies in my whole life, master."

"They are a good looking bunch, but they cost a pretty penny, Sergei. Any one of them cost ten times more than I paid that nasty little German dealer that sold you to me years ago, even though I admit you were a mighty good looking buck back when I first bought you."

"Inflation, master," Sergei smiled.

"Even taking inflation into account, any one of these pieces of slave flesh would bring three times more on the block than you could of in your prime. Admit it, Sergei, they're better looking, better hung, and better built than you ever were."

"Yes, master," Sergei chuckled. "They certainly are, but they don't have my years and years of experience in pleasing an exacting master."

"Maybe not, but I'll take care of that deficiency very shortly. On the other hand, they don't have mouths that run on and on either," I replied.

"No, master," Sergei replied, getting the message he was reaching the limits of proper slave protocol with a master, no matter how long they had lived together.

The crated slaves were rapidly becoming more and more active, stretching within the confines of their cramped cages and opened eyes were beginning to take in their new environment. I handed Sergei the keys to their cages and indicated he should proceed getting them lined up and standing on their own two feet so we could look them over.

Sergei reached down to the belt around the form fitting pants and shortened turtle-neck shirt I generally had him wear around the estate if we were expecting visitors and unhooked his multi-bladed slave whip, similar to the one Santos seemed to prefer back on the Greek island. With a sharp crack of the whip, he introduced himself as the head estate steward who would be in charge of them as their chief overseer from now on. Whipping off his turtle-necked shirt to expose his tall metal slave collar and his ringed tits, he explained that he himself was a slave so he was well aware of all the tricks and chicanery slaves were capable of, and that he ran a tight ship with lots of discipline: whippings with his own slave whip (waving it in the air for them to see) for the slightest mistakes or any hesitancy whatsoever in fulfilling an order. They were to respond to him by a simple "Yes, sir" or "No, sir" befitting his position over them. All food, water, getting to piss and shit, and alleviating their sex needs were earned privileges and would only be allowed with express permission of him or the master, and most slaves were whipped with a Mylar whip at least once a day whether they did anything wrong or not - all slaves were routinely whipped because they were slaves and needed to be reminded daily of their obligations - but much more severe beatings would be added if any problems were encountered with the slave during the course of a given day. Problems were defined as not demonstrating total subservience to their master or him at all times, talking too much or without permission, any looks or actions that could be interpreted as resembling resistance or not wanting to do a given act, and any act that didn't demonstrate the slave wanted to please the master to the best of his ability. They were not allowed to have any sex outlets or even touch their bodies in any way without direct permission from their owner, Mr. Parsimi, who had been kind enough to buy their miserable bodies for his use here at the estate. Sergei added that no slave ever wore clothes while on the estate, but would be dressed if they were taken off-grounds for one reason or another in the same type of clothes they first saw him in: turtle-necked shirts to hide their slave collars and tit rings cut off below their chest to best expose their abdominal muscles, and pants especially designed to flaunt their big baskets like the pants he had on right now. Their bodies would be used for a lot of manual work around the estate, generally under his supervision, for serving as litter bearers for the master when he desired that type of transportation, and, of course, for his sexual pleasure or the pleasure of anyone they were loaned out to. They were to keep themselves in top physical shape at all times and toward that end they would be exercised regularly if the manual work assigned or carrying the heavy litter did not keep their physiques perfect. Any backsliding from their training would not be tolerated, but would result in quick shipment back to Guiliano Import's Training Facilities.

Sergei was pleased this last statement brought a visible shudder to each and every slave being addressed.

"Just because I'm wearing a pair of pants now doesn't mean I've forgotten I'm a slave just like you. So I know how you think. I understand how you feel. I know you better than you know yourselves, you bastards. So don't think you can pull any wool over this slave's eyes," he stated, looking each slave straight in the eye. "If you try it, you'll end up with a body beaten so badly no one would give a lira for you, let alone waste the cost of feeding your body. On the other hand, you cooperate with me and your master, you give your whole being to everything you're told to do, whether it cleaning out a pig pen or taking it up the ass, and you'll manage to have a reasonably happy and fulfilling life just like I have."

"Well said, Sergei," I said rather warmly. "We do seem to enjoy our life together, don't we," I added, "and I still enjoy bedding you down. Which reminds me, you better tell them you'll probably be using their bodies now and then for your own pleasure."

"Yes, master," Sergei beamed at my praise. "You're most generous."

With a quick command and a sharp crack of his whip over the slave nearest him, Sergei had each new slave pick up and carry his cage to a storage room before moving them into the slave quarters for their thorough cleaning, obviously convinced they were fully capable now of carrying their heavy cages rather than waiting until later. Before all the cages had been hefted and carried away, each slave had tasted Sergei's biting whip on numerous parts of their body - a ritual Sergei utilized to establish his authority over them in all things right from the very beginning.

With 20 minutes after the truck had first delivered them, there wasn't a trace of the slaves or their cages visible from the main house. This was by design, of course. The slave quarters, totally soundproofed, were semi-underground, far out of sight of the main house or anyone visiting it.

That night, I had Sergei bring me two of the new purchases I had only hurriedly examined when I had bought them - the huge muscular blond from the Ukraine and the equally well built pure black from Chad in central Africa. Both were sparkling clean now, refreshed after a thorough bath and plenty of slave chow and a fresh watering, and both had been cleansed out and completely lubricated by Sergei in preparation for the night's activities. Sergei had also 'polished' both slaves with a light coat of body oil which made their skin glisten in the soft light of my quarters.

As they entered my quarters, totally nude except for the restraining tape and antiseptic cream over their newly installed tit rings, they immediately sank to their knees in obeisance with their collared necks bowed and their knees wide spread to best display their sexual organs.

"As you requested, Master," Sergei said indicating the two kneeling slaves attached by their collars to his leash. "Do you wish me to stay for supervision, Master?"

"Yes, Sergei. I really don't know these slaves well enough to trust them yet."

"Yes, master," Sergei said as he removed the leashes and retreated over to a corner with his head bowed but with his hand gripping his ever-ready slave whip.

Since neither slave spoke Italian yet, I spoke to them in English in which they understood simple commands from their training back on the Guiliano Island.

"You," I said pointing to the Ukrainian slave. "Suck me," I commanded.

Instantly, the Ukrainian crawled forward on his knees as I opened my robe, and swallowed my organ to the root in one gulp before suctioning it with hollowed cheeks for all he was worth. I moaned at the warm pleasurable feeling of his throat massaging my shaft and ran my hand through his thick, blond hair. His throat muscles seemed to seize my organ as he closed around it, massaging it vigorously and then he ran his tightened lips up and down by shaft, gripping it tightly in the process. Before I knew it, I shot a huge load down his throat. He never once faltered, but instead slurped and swallowed until every drop of my large discharge was residing in his stomach. Once the last discharge was down his throat, he swiftly cleaned by shaft with his tongue until it was completely clean.

"Thank you, master," he said humbly in English in a most sincere and soft, pleasing voice.

I let my robe slide to the floor as I ran my hand through his hair again.

"Would you like to fuck me now, master?" the Ukrainian slave invitedly asked as he again resumed a kneeling position with his genitals in full display.

"I'll need to recharge after that draining, slaveboy," I replied, "but I'm sure my steward would be happy to fuck you."

"Yes, master," both the steward and the Ukrainian said at once, the steward quickly moving over from his corner position peeling off his skin tight pants in the process (as a slave he wasn't allowed any underwear or shoes, steward or not), while the Ukrainian slave moved forward from his kneeling position.

"On my back, master, or on all fours?" the Ukrainian asked to make sure he was complying with my wishes.

"Hands and knees, slave. I can see how you take to the fucking better that way," I responded.

"Yes, master," the Ukrainian responded as he quickly assumed the commanded position, spreading his knees wide to again best expose his open hole.

Sergei just as quickly entered the hole his entire length, giving the slave under him no chance to adjust to the large intrusion. Instantly, he was pumping in and out of the hole, plunging the full length with each stroke but being careful not to grab the slave's tits beneath him.

As Sergie pistoned away into the slave's asshole, I studied the Ukrainian's beautiful face. It changed slowly from a grimace of pain at first entry to a look of resigned acceptance as his ass stretched itself fully open and finally to a look of sublime pleasure as Sergei continued plunging full length into the boy beneath him.

I hadn't read this boy's provenance yet and this was a good chance to do it.

"Male, age 20: 6'0" tall, 215 pounds: penis: 8x4 flaccid, 10x5 erect. Blond, blue-eyed Ukrainian acquired by our agents over 15 months ago from a German dealer specializing in local purchases, mainly rural, around Kiev. Boy sold at age 18 by aged "parents" who had taken homeless boy into their home (along with 15 other homeless boys) previously living on the streets of Kiev. Once in new home, fed and clothed well, but all educational efforts were directed at training in servile tasks thought to be marketable when children came of age and were fully developed. Hence, boy, totally illiterate even now, was taught waiting tables, cleaning tasks, gardening, animal management, and sheer manual labor as he developed to full musculature. After full sexual maturation, sold to German dealer in Kiev who began limited training in sexual skills for both heterosexual and homosexual markets, leasing the boy out, at one point, for two months to a local movie producer who wanted a live-in stud for her and her friend's personal amusement. Serving successfully on this assignment, he was then leased out to two other movie producers, this time male, who also wanted a live-in slave for their use for a two-month trial period. When returned, the two movie producers tried to buy him outright, but was outbid by our

agent whereupon he was promptly shipped to our training center. Thirteen months in training, yielding a slave who is totally accepting of his status in life, happy in his role of serving others, and should adjust well to any and all demands of a future owner. Very healthy and disease resistant with excellent attitude toward future placement as owned property. Price $290,000."

I looked down at the property being described, now being thoroughly fucked by my steward. He was dripping profusely and his deep blue eyes had a content look of total satisfaction.

"Enough, Sergei," I ordered.

As the steward withdrew his enormous twitching shaft from the Ukrainian's hole, he looked frustrated that he hadn't been allowed to shoot, but said nothing of course, and quickly resumed a kneeling position. The Ukrainian slave remained in place, not having been ordered to move.

"Sergei, fuck the black boy now - again riding the boy's back so I can study his reactions."

"Yes, master," Sergei responded as he immediately moved to the black slave telling him to get on all fours with a crack of his whip and promptly entered the slave full length with no preliminaries. The black gasped at the quick entry, churned his butt vigorously to ease the penetration, and then eased his knees even wider to stretch his hole. When Sergei was almost all the way in, the black pushed his butt back onto the invading shaft to aid in the complete ravishment of his hole.

"There's one eager slave," I laughed as the black again struggled to make sure all of Sergei's staff was completely in him and Sergei began pumping him rapidly, this time determined to reach orgasm as quickly as possible.

"Yes, master," Sergei grunted as the pace of his pistoning increased dramatically until the poor black was being scooted forward with each stroke of Sergei's giant organ. "May I shoot, master?" Sergei asked.

"Not yet, Sergei. Maybe later in the evening."

"Yes, master," Sergei responded, slowing the pace of his fucking considerably to avoid an action his master wouldn't allow at this point.

The black slave's shaft had swollen to full erection and was dripping copiously as the fucking continued. He looked at me pleadingly, but I shook my head negatively whereupon he compliantly gritted his teeth, closed his black eyes, and strained his muscles to avoid shooting off himself.

With both Sergei and the black slave struggling to obey their master and avoid cumming as the fucking continued, I casually studied the black's provenance, enjoying the power inherent in the slaves' struggle to control their bodies due simply to my whim of the moment.

"Male, 20 years old, 6'0", 230 pounds; Penis: 8x5 flaccid; 12x5.5 erect. Acquired in Chad slave markets by our agents 12 months ago when slave was 20 years of age. Being sold by third owner to date to acquire funds for purchase of another similar slave 18-years-old, an age more in line with owner's preferences, i.e., a trade-in. Had served third owner as basic house servant, doing all cleaning, cooking and laundry, as well as sole bed buck for widowed owner and his 16-year-old son. This slave was the son of a slave couple owned by first owner who sold him off at 10 to an elderly couple needing personal assistance and househouse chores done for them,. When they died eight years later, he was sold to third owner at age 18 who bought him as general house servant and personal catamite. Took to training at our facilities readily and with no difficulties, telling trainers this was the best life he had ever experienced so far with its easily understood rules, clear discipline standards, and expectations that were predictable. Eager to be sold to new owner now that he is fully trained after only six months. Should adjust well to any new owner who sets clear boundaries and expectations of behavior and who is rigid in enforcing discipline at all times. Has no concept of freedom or individual decision-making due to being born into slavery. Sales Price: $220,000 due to surplus of blacks at this time in world markets.

The black being discussed was sweating profusely on the floor beneath me as he struggled to keep from ejaculating from the constant stimulation Sergei was providing up his hole.

"Keep your prick in him, but reach around and jerk the black off but time it so you both cum at the same time, Sergei," I directed.

Sergei smiled broadly, happy that at last his master was going to allow him to alleviate his overwhelming need, and quickly reached around the slave he had mounted and began stroking the huge shaft.

The black slave again looked up pleadingly at me with this new stimulation and this time I nodded affirmatively whereupon he broke into a huge smile which lit up his face as almost instantly he began to buck and whinny as he shot strand after strand of thick, hot cum onto the floor beneath him, gasping for air with each new emission. Sergei plunged all the way in, froze into rigidity as he emptied his balls deep into the black's bowels, and, after several spastic jerks, collapsed on the black slave's back.

"Well, that was quite a show," I commented as both slaves, wet with sweat, continued panting.

"Yes, master. Thank you, master," Sergei muttered.

"Both of you, up on your feet. And you," I said pointing to the black slave, "assume display position. I want to look you over now that your balls are emptied."

"Yes, master," the Chadian said, quickly assuming the commanded position the minute Sergei was off his back.

I looked him over thoroughly, studying the high cheek bones, his deep heavily lashed black eyes, his smooth, sweaty skin, his powerful musculature, his puffed-out over-developed pectorals topped with the taped tits, and then ran my hand down his ridged abdominal muscles, his thick muscular thighs, his muscular but heavily fleshed butt, and finally, the large ball sac, now noticeably unswollen, and his very thick but unusually smooth long penis, now protruding far out from his body for very easy handling thanks to the recently installed genital band. He quivered and shuddered a few times as I stroked his body from the excitement of being handled, but otherwise remained absolutely still for my inspection. His shaft was already once again fully erect, a result of my handling no doubt as well as the months of training in effectively responding to an owner's inspection. His broad smile when given permission to ejaculate had never left his face and he gave every impression he loved being fondled and inspected.

"What a buy!" I exclaimed. "Only $220,000 for a boy this well trained. That's little more than I paid for you, Sergei, decades ago."

"Yes, master. And he's extremely handsome, at least in my eyes," Sergei ventured.

"That he is, Sergei. The epitome of masculine beauty."

"I don't know what epitome means, master, but he sure is a looker," Sergei added, "and he obviously enjoys being fucked as you probably noticed, master."

"That I'm going to find out shortly, Sergei. Take them both back to the slave quarters and clean them out completely. Then bring them back freshly lubricated. I'm going to bed this black down tonight and you can have the Ukrainian blond to do with as you please. I'm feeling so horny now I think I'll fuck this black two or three times before the sun rises if all goes well."

"Yes, master," Sergei said as he quickly snapped the leashes on the neck collars of the two slaves and headed for the slave's quarters. In 10 minutes, he reentered the room with both of the slaves following on their leashes. He fastened the leash of the black to my bed, and led the Ukrainian slave to a small rug over in the corner where slaves often rutted on the floor for their master's entertainment and where Sergei slept himself when ordered to his master's bedroom and wasn't in use in his master's bed.

Within two weeks, all of the tit piercings had healed with no problems and now each of the new slaves were adjusting to the new and strange sensation of tit rings bouncing off their bodies at the slightest provocation. By this time, each of them had "settled" into their new cages in the slave quarters, had learned to appreciate Sergei's strict discipline and proper efficient organization of their time, and were busily exercising each day at assigned manual labor around the estate to keep their bodies in top shape. The food and accommodations were good, compared to what they were used to, and their duties pleasing the sexual needs of both their new master and his steward were certainly comfortably well within the boundaries of what their training had led them to expect. They expected their usage in this area to increase once their new master began to entertain his friends and show off his new litter which was scheduled to arrive shortly.

Each morning, the steward milked each of them when they first arose, gathering up their sizable morning output into a one-liter thermos café so that its natural warmth could be retained on its trip to the master's breakfast table. Their master, Sergei told them, enjoyed a cup or so of warm cum with his breakfast not only because he liked the taste and texture of fresh cum, but because it was thought to be an effective anti-aging agent if you ingested enough of it. Toward that end, he saved the rest to use as a condiment or sauce while eating his lunch and dinner, dependent on what was on the menu that day.

Any cum left in the café was sprinkled over their own slave chow for added flavor and protein, so none got wasted. Sergei told them every time they chowed down, they were getting a little taste of each other as a special bond between them. Although any flavoring to their monotonous feed was welcome, they were most appreciative of the chance to empty their balls each morning and sincerely thanked both Sergei and their master each time Sergei milked them.

"Thank the master for me, sir," was a common heart-felt response each time one of the slaves shot load after load into the fancy café under the direction of Sergei's busy fingers. So far, it was about their only chance to alleviate their every present sexual needs and, knowing how painful overstuffed balls could be from being caged so long in the Guiliano's island's sales department, they were all the more appreciative.

The litter arrived a day earlier than scheduled and the eight new slaves were immediately put to the final assembly of the contraption and then chained by their newly installed tit rings to the poles themselves.

"If you let the litter fall, you're going to get dragged down with it, and your tits are really going to feel that," Sergei warned as he fastened either the left or right tit ring to the poles, dependent on which side of the litter the slave was stationed. "I don't think I need to tell you to make certain the litter is in the correct position at all times, no matter what the terrain," he laughed as the last slave's tit-ring was snapped to the chain connected to the poles. "You're going to feel the weight of the chain on your tit-ring to start with, and when you get going, it's going to bounce up and down on those rings, so you're going to feel it through and through with every step you take. It should keep you all fully erect at all times - that's the ideal - so concentrate on getting your prick hard all the time. That's the way litter bearers are supposed to be to show well. Those rings vibrating and pulling on your tits when you're trotting should cause everyone of you to be hard all the time easily enough, but when you're just standing, you're going to have to concentrate on keeping that prick just as hard as it was when you are trotting and the rings are tugging away on you. Any failure in that area and you'll feel the whip on your body until you learn how to keep it up all the time, no matter what."

"You understand, slaves?" he cracked the whip over their heads for emphasis. "Up and hard all the time, no matter what."

"Yes, master," they all responded, already erect from the unique tit stimulation of the rings weighed down by the chain, not knowing whether the feeling was pleasant or not at this point.

"We'll start your training with the litter empty until you get used to that load and how it feels on your shoulders, especially when we get you up to speed. After that, we'll load it down with about 500 pounds of sandbags so you can see what carrying the master and a guest or two would be like. Then, we'll teach you how to lift it smoothly even when fully loaded and how to crouch down becomingly beside it when you're resting so that your bodies still display well."

With that, Sergei worked the slaves hour after hour, day after day, hefting the litter smoothly, trotting together in a totally coordinated fashion with one slave designated the lead slave each day so they all learned how to serve this function, serving in all positions of the litter so they were familiar with the different strains on the muscles unique to each position, and finally, building up their wind to take the long fast runs their master might require.

At first, each slave's leashed tit became red and inflamed from the constant irritation, but within a week or so they toughened, although all tits got noticeably larger as the resultant swelling never really left, but their bodies developed even more musculature - waists got thinner, hips more rounded, and shoulders, thighs, and arms even more massive as the intense training continued. When running in coordinated step with their mates, each felt their banded genitals swaying back and forth in perfect harmony, and each step was felt as the tit rings swung back and forth from their swollen tits, again in a totally coordinated fashion. Within three weeks, the team performed error free and could run mile after mile at a fast pace without stumbling or collapsing from lack of wind. At full pace, their feet slapped the pavement like horse's hooves, their tit rings jingled on their litter leashes in harmony, and even their steady gasping for air was done rhythmically like the chugging of a well-functioning steam engine. All eight slaves had learned, with the motivation of Sergei's frequent beatings, how to keep themselves fully erect at all times, even when the tit rings weren't stimulating them and most of the slaves now found themselves hard and dripping whenever they were leashed to the litter. Sergei, had, in effect, conditioned them to be hard whenever the litter was present, a fact clearly established when the slaves started to become erect the minute they even saw the litter, long before they were leashed to it by their tit rings.

Sergei urged his master to try it out when convenient as soon as the extensive training was complete.

I did and was more than pleased with the final result. The slaves lifted my weight easily and smoothly up to their full height and smoothly increased their speed until a fast trot was maintained mile after mile around the estate's roads. I invited Sergei up with me on the second round to see how they handled the weight of two grown adults. Again, the operation went very smoothly, although the panting increased in volume and frequency noticeably, but not enough to slow the conveyance in any way.

Several days later, I decided to have an endurance trial and, with both Sergei and I aboard, we ordered a fast run - not trot - for a good ten miles. The slaves never faltered or stumbled despite their desperate gasps for air. Sergei's "encouragement" to keep up the pace during the last two miles with his whip constantly lashing over their bodies and the muted groans after each lash only added to the excitement of the run. But at the end of the ten mile fast run, the slaves literally collapsed as far as their tit leashes would allow, choking and gasping trying to get air into their tortured lungs. Sergei jumped off the litter and whipped each one unmercifully, cursing them for being lazy, unappreciative whores as well as worthless slaves not worth what it cost to feed them, but even with this, they could go no further no matter how hard he laced into their bodies with his painful Mylar whip. They didn't have the strength left to scream from the horrific beating, and, for once, their omnipresent erections were gone.

"Well, now we know the limits of the contraption," I laughed as the slaves moaned in agony from Sergei's severe beatings and their irritated tits, throbbing in pain from the constant stretching of their leashes. "I'd say eight miles max with a full load at a fast run; ten with just one person aboard. But at a reasonable trot, it seems they can go mile after mile with no trouble, especially if just one's aboard. But even with two, I doubt if they'd wear out within a day. Well done, Sergei."

"Thank you, master. I'm not sure further training will pay off or not, master. Their lungs are the problem, master, not their muscles.

I can see where horses have a big advantage with those big lungs of theirs," he mused as the slaves around him continued gasping for air and moaning from the residual pain of Sergei's beatings.

"You slaves should thank your master for putting you to this test," Sergei suggested pointedly, raising his whip once again.

"Thank you, master. Thank, you, master," was choked out between gasps with their eyes pleading that they not be whipped further.

"And I should think you would want to thank my slave Sergei for training you to this level," I replied.

"Thank you, sir. Thank, you, Sergei sir," they all again bleated, still trying to get their breath.

With a crack of his whip, Sergei ordered the exhausted slaves to their feet, but then ordered only a slow walk back to the main door of the estate with both he and his master aboard the heavy litter. The slaves managed to again smoothly raise the litter to full height and, still gasping for air, walked the litter in a smooth coordinated fashion back to the main house despite the pain wracking their bodies from the fearsome beating. When they knelt down together to lower the litter to ground height, each one hung his head in proper subservience with his knees spread wide to display his once again fully erect organ.

"Didn't take them long to recover, Sergei," I said, pointing to their erect dripping organs.

"No, master," Sergei responded. "They're all ready for your bed tonight if you so desire."

"Let's see," I said looking them over carefully. "I'll take the Arabian black and the Australian tonight. I haven't fucked them for over a week now."

"Yes, master," Sergei said as, with a crack of his whip, he had the team move the litter to the storage shed and then moved the slaves themselves to the slave quarters where he would supervise their baths, feeding, and preparation for the night's activities.

There were only two provenances I hadn't studied yet of my newly acquired team of litter bearers. One was the American black and the other was the 21-year-old Asian slave Guiliano Imports had bought in Hong Kong. I turned my attention to the Asian slave first.

"*Male, Asian, 21-years-old: 6'0"; 195 pounds; Penis: 7.5 x 4.2 flaccid, 11x4.5 erect. This slave is of pure Chinese stock and was first sold into slavery in the province of Nanking in the Chinese mainland when he was 18 years of age by roving slave catchers who had overtaken his small village the night before. He, along with five other villagers (4 females and himself) were shackled and caged and then transported by closed truck to Hong Kong, where they were sold at discount prices to a underground Chinese slave dealer who frequently bought goods, both human and other, off of these roving thieves at bargain prices. The four female slaves were quickly sold to local merchants in a discrete auction, but the male was sold privately to a mining concern who promised to keep him in close confinement and "break" him into slavery. A year later, his physique was spectacular from the extreme hard work in the mines, and the frequent beatings and other punishments had fully acclimated him to his new status. His owners decided to cut a quick profit on him by selling him to a brothel catering to both male and female customers in the Kowtoon district. The brothel master there trained him in pleasing both female and male customers and soon, due to his youth, vigor, splendid good looks, and magnificent physique, he was a popular favorite, especially among the female customers who found his ability to withhold any debilitating orgasm until they commanded it, was worth whatever they had to pay for his services. When he reached the age of 20, our agents offered his owner a purchase price equal to his earnings in the house over the next five years. Since they were well aware most brothel slaves decline in performance well before five years of heavy service, they quickly sold him whereupon he was shipped to our island for training. Training took 11 months without complications and the slave seems most content with his present status, claiming (probably rightfully) that he is better treated and respected for his unique abilities and showy body than he would have been back in his home village where only farm labor is valued. Should adjust to any and all demands placed upon him by a future owner. Purchase price: $295,000 due to age.*"

I quickly went to the next provenance.

"*Male, 19-year-old mulatto; 6'0", 220 pounds; Penis: 8x5 flaccid; 11.5x5.5 erect. Born to a black prostitute operating in Dallas, Texas, USA, who conceived him with a white customer (exact customer unknown). Raised in numerous short-term foster homes in the Texas child welfare system until he was sentenced at age 15 to Juvenile Corrections for drug dealing and*

*two counts of pimping. Released six months later on probation, but terms
of probation broken when he was 17, again allegedly dealing in illicit drugs
and new counts of working within an illegal escort service catering to adult
females. Sentenced to Texas Correctional Prison where his "adjustment"
primarily consisted of selling himself to other inmates for small favors. Our
agents, who keep close contact with this warden, bought this male outright on
his 18th birthday, the same time the warden signed a death certificate for him
along with ownership papers to our agent. Sent to island for training which
was completed in 15 months, requiring a long period of initial adjustment to
slave status and expected duties of a male slave but resulted in a magnificent
physical development. Now fully acclimated to new status as owned
property, adjusts well to structured environments requiring little decision-
making, and responses well to authority. Enjoys admiration his body receives
from prospective purchasers and is eager to please them regardless of their
gender despite his basic heterosexual preferences (but understanding fully
a slave has no preferences when it comes to performance). Should make an
excellent adjustment to new owner if proper discipline is utilized. Purchase
price: $290,000 due to mixed racial lines."*

Interesting, I thought. Here was a slave who had done nothing
for the past 15 months but get fucked up his butt, suck other men
off on command, fuck other men on command, get milked by men
over and over, and let men paw and probe every part of his body as
ordered. Yet they still mentioned a "basic heterosexual preference."
Some guys never give in, he thought to himself, no matter what
happens to them or how much they're tossed around by other men.

Just this morning, the mulatto slave happened to be tit-
leashed right next to me on a litter ride. I had the litter bars at their
top level (the bars supported the roof of the litter and hence I was
suspended beneath the bearer's shoulders). At that time, I had
admired his beautifully muscular physique, his handsome face,
but especially his light tan skin, highlighted by the copious sweat
running down his cheeks, over his pecs, dripping off his tits and the
end of his shaft, running down his stomach, back, and rump, giving a
glowing appearance to his smooth hide. His tits were large and well-
shaped, having grown considerably since he had been ringed, and
his large organ was fully erect the entire trot, his equipment swaying
back and forth in perfect coordination with his fellow litter bearers.
Even his panting, quite noticeable at the trot I had ordered them to
maintain, was smooth and soothing, lacking the desperate gasping

that sounded rather ugly when they were ordered to a prolonged running pace. When I had reached out of the litter to stroke his sweaty body as he worked, he lifted his head briefly and let out a dazzling smile, letting me know he appreciated this special attention from his master, before quickly assuming the normal position of a head bowed as low as his tall neck collar would allow.

It was hard to believe he wasn't really into the only type of sex he was allowed at the estate if the provenance was right, I knew such slaves were relatively rare in that most slaves quickly learned to like the new forms of sex demanded of them, but often fun to fuck when you knew, deep down inside, they sort of resented it, no matter how much training they'd had. It would be fun to watch another slave fuck him so he could study his face and see if any remnant of that old "preference" was actually still there. I sort of doubted it - for over a year now, his only source of sexual release had been with other men. I doubted if he even remembered what a women was like anymore. I looked forward to questioning this mulatto slave as to whether he resented being "used" by men like he was regularly. He might even ask him if he wanted to be sold off to a mistress. Yes, that was it! A much better test. If he was eager to be sold as a mistress' house stud (a growing market in sophisticated circles I understood), it meant that old "preference" was still part of him.

That evening I had Sergei cleanse the American mulatto slave and bring him up to my suite in the manor house. As Sergei led him into my quarters by his neck leash, he was fully erect with a drop of pre-cum showing on the end of his large swollen circumcised prick. He promptly knelt in his master's presence with his knees wide spread, his hands in back of his neck collar, and with this chest thrust out to best display his body. Sergei had given him a coat of light oil on his hairless shaved body so it gleamed in the artificial light, highlighted by his bright metal collar, genital band, and tit rings which showed up well on his light tan smooth skinned body. Both slaves had their heads bowed awaiting instructions.

"On your hands and knees, slave, with your knees spread wide," I ordered the mulatto.

"And you, Sergei, fuck this slave thoroughly until I tell you to stop. No shooting off, Sergei, but you ram it in him good. I want to study how this slave takes to a good fucking."

"Yes, master," both slaves answered as they assumed the commanded positions.

Sergei inserted his huge shaft slowly up the mulatto's lubricated butt hole, twisting it as he entered, until he had all 12 inches fully up the boy's stretched hole. He waited briefly and then began a slow steady plunging of his shaft in and out of the hole, bringing it all the way back each time until he was almost out and then plunging it back with great force before repeating the cycle over and over.

I studied the mulatto's face as he was being deep fucked. At first entry, he gritted his teeth and grimaced until Sergei was all the way in him, wiggling his butt a little to best accommodate the intruding shaft. But I saw no indication of resentment whatsoever - in fact the mulatto seemed to be pushing himself onto the shaft at times to gain full penetration. When the fucking motions actually started, he again shifted his butt around a little but mainly in order to tense his butt muscles to grip the shaft within him. The mulatto's own shaft, quivering in full erection beneath him, begin dripping profusely onto the carpet beneath him. As I saw the mulatto's slave work his ass muscles, I knew he was gripping and massaging Sergei's shaft - he was, in effect, "milking" Sergei's shaft as he was being fucked.

I chuckled to myself. Such wanton licentiousness was more typical of an experienced male whore getting his jollies with a client than a slave boy resenting every moment of his rape. It certainly wasn't behavior you'd expect of a slave "preferring" fucking a female and resenting everything else he was forced to do. I suspected the provenance of this slave provided at the time of his sale was considerably off the mark.

"You like being fucked?" I asked the mulatto.

"Yes, master," the slave quickly responded, panting from his 'milking' efforts on Sergei's shaft. "A lot, master," he sighed as he again stretched his hole further onto the shaft plunging into him.

I reached down and felt his balls.

"Sergei, didn't you milk this boy this morning?" I asked as I squeezed the firm, swollen balls, obviously chock full of cum.

"Yes, master. I drained him completely no more than 10 hours ago. But this slave boy recharges fast, master. He's usually dripping again by noon each and every day, no matter how much I pump out of him that morning.

"Pull out of him, Sergei. I want to fuck him myself now."

"Yes, master," Sergei responded as he withdrew inch by inch from the stretched hole, his own prick quivering in need, covered with ass slime and lubricants. "You want me to lube him up again, master?"

"No," I answered as I took Sergei's place on the boy's back and quickly inserted by own phallus well up the boy's anus.

"Now, slave, you milk my shaft in you just like you were working on Sergei's. There's no use for me doing all the work. You bring me off with your ass muscles."

"Yes, master," the mulatto said without hesitation as I felt his ass muscles cramp around my shaft and begin rhythmic contractions that felt exactly like fingers milking my prick as I remained as still as I could under such stimulation.

I reached beneath the slave and grabbed his own pulsating prick and began stroking it.

"No shooting off until I give you permission, slave," I whispered in his ear as I timed my stroking of his prick with the pace of his own ass contractions on my prick.

The mulatto slave broke out in a sweat all over his body as he struggled to control shooting off and his breathing became ragged as his own ass muscles picked up the pace of their fierce contractions in the task of 'milking' me, drawing my own prick into his body more and more with each contraction.

Within minutes, I felt my own discharge racing up by penis and I leaned down and whispered in the slave's ear that he could discharge when he felt me do so, and then reared up as spasm after spasm tore through my body with each new discharge deep into the slave's rectum, raking my hands across the slave's back in the process.

"Thank you, master, thank you," the mulatto practically screamed as his body stiffened and he discharged buckets of steaming hot cum on the carpet beneath him, his stomach, his chest, and his chin and even his face as his prick waved around desperately dispelling his huge load.

I left my prick in him as he continued bucking in his post-orgasmic reactions and said, "How would you like to be sold to a mistress?"

"You're going to sell me, master?" the mulatto asked, terrified. "Please, master, don't sell this slave. I'll be better, master. I'll do anything you want, master, but please don't sell me off, master," he spit out, tears welling in his eyes.

"I was told you preferred serving women, slave boy," I responded quietly, my prick still buried deep within him.

The slave looked perplexed, then puzzled, and finally anxious.

"No, master. No, master. I don't want a mistress, master."

"Slaves have no choice of who owns them, master or mistress, slave boy. You know that, so you watch your tongue. And slaves don't 'want' anything for themselves. They only 'want' what best suits their owner - you know that. You'll have to be punished for such stupid talk, slave boy."

"Yes, master, I know, master," the mulatto replied, openly crying now.

"You'd rather be fucked like this than be fucking a nice mistress?" I taunted him.

"Yes, master," he tearfully responded. "Yes, master," he repeated.

"Well, you certainly respond like you like to get fucked by a master," I teased him as I rubbed his own hot cum all over his belly and chest. "You can't shoot a load like this if you don't like it, I wouldn't think."

"No master, I love to get fucked, especially when I'm allowed to shoot off like you just let me, master. Nothing I like better, master."

"Have you forgotten how good it is to fuck a women, slaveboy, even though, with a mistress, she'd be calling all the shots?"

"Master, it's been so long I can't even remember, master. Never even saw a women in prison, master, and, since I was sold off to that company you bought me from, I only fucked three or four slave women as part of my training but that was under heavy direction, master."

"Yes, but wouldn't you prefer servicing a mistress than servicing all of us around here?" I put to him bluntly. "I can arrange it, you know, by selling you to a good mistress who is looking for a likely stud to service her at her whim."

"Yes, master, I know you can sell me off to anyone you want anytime, but, master, I beg you not too. I've never been happier in my whole life than since you bought me, master, and I've learned to like servicing men better than anything I can remember, master. I get more excited, master, and shoot off bigger loads, master, than any sex I can remember before I was taught how to service masters," he said with a serious and studied look. "Yes, master," he concluded, "I guess I'm just a natural man whore now if you want me to tell you the honest truth."

"That's exactly what I want you to do," I said, feeling my prick becoming erect again while still in his butt. "I won't sell you to a mistress, slave boy, if you give us everything you've got in that pretty body of yours," I continued.

"I will, master. I'll give you everything I've got, master. I love you master," he added for good measure. "My life with you is better than anything I ever imagined possible, master," he slave said, breaking into sobbing once again.

"That's exactly why I going to fuck you again, you half-black whore, before I change my mind."

Sergei chuckled from his kneeling position in the corner, happy the slave under his supervision had pleased his master.

As I turned the mulatto slave over, motioning for him to place his legs over his shoulder, I resumed a long leisurely fuck of this new property. Apparently, the provenance provided by Guiliano Imports was sadly out of date!

———

The Chinese slave was still kneeling in the corner, head bowed awaiting instructions. I had completely forgotten him until I finally finished fucking the mulatto for the second time and, after resting a bit, looked over to Sergei, kneeling beside the Chinese slave.

I ordered him to display position and took my time in thoroughly inspecting his body - much more thoroughly than when I first bought him. The slave had been leashed closest to me on the opposite side of the litter this morning and so I couldn't help but notice his magnificent musculature and exuding masculine sexuality at that time. After examining every square inch of his body, including pinching his swollen tits, cupping his large ringed balls, stroking his long thick cock and opening his hole with my fingers to test his tightness there, I couldn't find one fault with this slave's body no matter how hard I looked for even one simple blemish. His Asian features only added to his handsomeness. His beautiful brown eyes were slanted slightly upward to give an almost feline look to his otherwise rugged face and the yellow skin was doubly attractive when it was shiny with sweat, as it was in the slave's excitement of being examined by his master.

I ordered him to kneel again and then motioned for him to crawl toward me, pointing to my flaccid organ. Instantly, he understood he was to suck his master and promptly swallowed the entire organ down his throat and began massaging the shaft with his throat while he very gently lifted my balls with his hands and lightly gripped them to heighten the effect of his oral ministrations. Despite my previous activities, I felt myself hardening in his mouth and could actually feel my shaft inching its way down his open throat.

"Sergei," I ordered. "Mount him from the rear and fuck this slave while he's servicing me with his mouth."

"Yes, master," Sergei said, immediately crawling over to the slave's back and mounting him, then slowly inserting his own hard shaft up the slave's open hole.

The Chinese slave moaned softly as Sergei's shaft entered him, but never wavered in his mouth suctioning and massaging my shaft with his throat muscles. Quite the contrary, once Sergei started pounding into him, his own actions increased in intensity as if he had to swallow even more of me and he churned and contracted his throat muscles in perfect harmony to Sergei's pumping of his ass.

I reached down and grabbed the Chinese slave's tit-rings, tugging and twisting them until his tits were fully erect and swollen bright red. Then I squeezed them, rubbing them between my thumb and forefinger until they swelled ever bigger in my hand. The slave moaned again, and reaching down to place my hand around the slave's own erect organ, I found him dripping profusely, even more than when Sergei started fucking him. This slave obviously responded to tit play, I noted, and probably received considerable pleasure just being tit-leashed to the litter where his tits were under constant stimulation. He probably had trouble keeping from shooting off just being leashed that way.

"Oh," I moaned as I shot down the slave's throat, my third discharge that evening. The Chinese slave's throat muscles contracted around my shaft and milked the last drop out of me while Sergei continued pumping his ass.

"You can unload if you want now, Sergei," I allowed.

"Thank you, master," Sergei said, plunging deeply into the Chinese slave's ass and then stiffening as he discharged load after load deep into the slave boy beneath him. "Thank you, master," he repeated as he withdrew his still erect shaft, wet with cum and ass juices from the slave's stretched hole.

"And you can shoot now, slave," I said to the Chinese man, still rubbing his tits vigorously.

"Thank you, master. Thank you," the slave panted as he immediately began shooting hot cum out in spurt after spurt all over himself and some clear up on my hands still playing with his tits. A look of pure gratitude spread over his handsome face. "Thank you, master," he gasped out once again as he continued spurting cum.

When the Chinese slave had finally emptied his balls and had lifted himself up on his knees to give me easier access to his tits, I continued playing with them.

"You love having your tits played with, don't you slave?" I smiled at him.

"Yes, master. More than anything, master," he said, pushing his tits even further into my kneading fingers.

"You must have been in heaven when I had you ringed," I commented.

"Yes, master. I loved it, master. Now I'm excited all the time, master," he responded almost dreamily as I continued stimulating his tits.

"And you, of all the slaves I own for the litter, must love being leashed by your tits," I added.

"Yes, master. Every moment on the tit leash makes it difficult for me to control shooting off, master. Master, I'm always on the edge when I'm leashed to the litter, master."

"Good, but you keep yourself from shooting off while you're tit-leashed. You can only shoot off with my permission, slaveboy."

"Yes, master. I know, master. I always control myself, master," the slave assured me.

My friend, John Morgan, loved playing with a slave's tits as I recalled. He would love this Chinese tit freak. When I invited him for a visit to see my new litter in action, I would make sure he was given the Chinese slave for his personal servant and bed partner while he was visiting. Those two would really appreciate each other. I owned him an invitation anyway, especially after he had referred me to Guiliano Imports to start with.

"I'm going to have a small party to show off my litter, Sergei," I announced two days later. "Just a few close friends who would appreciate the novelty of the contraption and would probably love to take a demonstration ride now that you've got the slaves fully trained."

"Yes, master," Sergei responded, his head bowed low over his ever-present slave collar.

"I was thinking of no more than eight. That way each guest can pick out their own slave to serve them when they aren't on litter duty and we'd still have you as a spare."

"Yes, master. But what about your own needs when they are here?" Sergei politely asked.

"As I said, I've always got your body to amuse me - aged as it is."

"Yes, master. Of course, master." Sergei responded brightly, considering I had just made a crack about him getting older.

Without further ado, I sent out invitations to eight of my friends who shared my interest in the proper utilization of slaveboys in today's society and who had the means and wherewithal to make that utilization a reality. All discretely owned slaves of their own, carefully hidden away at their own retreats throughout the world, but none, to the best of my knowledge, had slaves trained to the litter. The novelty would amuse them.

With 24 hours, all had responded by phone that they would be delighted to visit and all were looking forward to a ride in my new litter. All planned to stay at least overnight in order to fully enjoy the litter slaves when they were "off the poles." Most said they would be bringing a slave or two of their own to help out, but I assured them it wouldn't be necessary. I thought the slaves I had on hand could handle their needs, no matter what they were. But they insisted, so I could hardly order them not to. As one of the guests put it, "we like to show off too, buddy!"

"Let's hope your new slaves are up to this new attack on their bodies," one of them joked over the phone. "If they are, my own slaves will be happy for the rest, I'm sure," he laughed.

John Morgan said he had heard from Eduardo Guiliano himself that I had purchased eight well hung slaves to train for carrying a Roman-style litter around my estate and that, since he hadn't heard back from me, Eduaro had assumed it was all working out fine. I told him it worked out better than I thought it would, and the stock I bought was damn good in pleasuring their master too. He laughed and said he looked forward to the visit where he could see about that "pleasuring" himself. He had been to the island himself only last week where he had traded one of his slaves in on a fresher, younger one who was a real looker.

"Got a great price on him too," John exclaimed. "Eduardo says there's a glut in the market right now and that prices are unusually low."

'Yes," I replied. "I was surprised how little I had to pay, considering the quality of the stock I purchased."

"Good," John replied. "I'll see you in a few days. Oh, by the way Aristo Mythos said to be sure and give you his regards," John added, right before he hung up.

———————

The day of the party arrived. All eight guests had arrived as scheduled, along with 14 of their slaves. Most of the guests had flown in, then rented a car with one of their slaves chauffeuring them to the estate while a second slave, if they had brought one, was stuffed into the boot. All the slaves arrived fully dressed in the standard slave outfit for traveling with their masters: turtle necked shirts that covered their collars, tight pants cut to display their ample baskets, and a simple pair of sandals or slip-on shoes over their bare feet. Judging from their walk, most had been butt plugged for the trip, probably to constantly remind them of their slave status while oust among free folk.

The minute each party arrived, the slaves, without being told, promptly stripped and stored their clothing in the cars. They kept their butt plugs inserted, however, and promptly kneeled at their master's feet, awaiting instructions.

I suggested the slaves be put under Sergei's supervision who would take them, with their master's permission, to the slaves' quarters for a thorough cleansing inside and out along with a series of enemas.

"Do the masters want their slave's butt plugs reinserted once they're cleansed?" Sergei asked humbly, kneeling with a lowered head at my side.

"No, have them clean if off thoroughly and then lock it in the car with their clothes - they'll need it for our return trip," one of the guests answered and the other guests all nodded in agreement. "I guess they'll get enough use in their hole to stay open pretty well without the plugs," he laughed and the other guests again nodded in agreement.

By early afternoon, all the guests had arrived, their slaves were cleansed and returned to the manor to attend their masters along with Sergei who was, along with the other slaves, kneeling alongside his master.

"Let's see this contraption you're so proud of," John Morgan said. "We all made the trip to see the damn thing in operation, so get it and that team of slaves you're so proud of out here where we can all take a little demonstration ride."

I had anticipated this, and just as John Morgan said this, the huge litter was sighted through the window rapidly making its way to the manor house at a fast trot. The guests rushed out of the room to the entry to study it up close. As the litter got closer, the guests could hear the tit leashes bouncing off the litter bars, the coordinated panting of the litter slaves that so resembled a steam engine in operation, and admired the huge erect penises, all banded for upmost protrusion, swaying together in perfect rhythm.

"My God. It's magnificent!" one guest exclaimed. "The slaves are all matched for height, weight, and physique. And, my God, even their pricks are the same size. Absolutely brilliant!"

"Well, they are about the same height and weight, but they do vary a little," I smiled, "and their pricks aren't quite the same when they're erect like they are whenever they're on duty this way, but they are matched for size when they're flaccid."

"I love the variation in their hides," another guest exclaimed. "About every color available in the markets these days A very nice touch."

"I think the most spectacular thing are those tit-leashes. A beautiful idea and so creative," another guest said. "It just reeks of total control, especially on tits that are already ringed and so nicely developed as a result of being ringed."

"The leashes are a nice touch," another guest admitted, "but banding their package tightly with a showy circlet like you've done to exhibit it so nicely is just perfect. That way, they all show well and it even makes their shafts swing in symphony with each other - it's a beautiful sight."

As the heavy ornate litter came to a halt right in front of them, the guests appreciated the heavy coordinated breathing, the quivering muscles in their magnificent bodies reacting to the load upon their shoulders, and the phalluses which remained erect even while standing still.

"Splendid - just splendid," another guests said as he ran his hand down the sweating body of the slave nearest him, the full-black from Chad. "But," he said, hefting up the ball sac of the slave and squeezing it, "how do you keep them hard all the time?"

"Lots of training," I responded, enjoying the compliments. "They get hard the minute they see the litter now and stay that way until we put it away. My slave trainer Sergei calls it 'Pavlovian conditioning' or some such thing. But Sergei's a Polish slave - he's always trying to play up the Eastern Europeans," I laughed. "At any rate, as you see for yourself," I added, motioning to all eight slaves' quivering erections, some with a drop of pre-cum at the end of their pricks, "it works."

"Now, who wants a ride first? We can handle two at a time easily enough."

John Morgan and another guest from England indicated they would like to be first, and smoothly placed themselves into the lowered litter. They were both big men and the total weight would be close to 550 pounds I thought.

I snapped by finger, nodding at the lead slave and the litter was hoisted smoothly onto the slaves' shoulders, and with another snap of my finger, I ordered "Around the lake and back at a moderate trot."

Instantly the litter glided down the road, picking up speed until the "moderate trot" speed they had been taught over and over was reached. The remaining guests marveled at how swiftly it sped out of sight and how smoothly it moved on the cushioning shoulders of the eight slaves.

The designated route was about a mile-and-a-half, so it wasn't long until the litter again came into sight. This time, the heavy panting of the slaves was audible hundreds of feet away and the sun reflected brightly off of their sweat-soaked bodies. When they returned and lowered the litter down smoothly, their heavy panting, totally coordinated, was most evident as was the sweat rolling off of their ringed tits, their massive pecs, their erect phalluses, and even down their muscular thighs.

"Glorious!" John and the other Englishman exclaimed.

"One of the best experiences I've had," the other Englishman explained.

"Guilo," John Morgan said excitedly, "It's a novel use of slaves that's a real pleasure - their struggling to maintain the pace; their heavy breathing all for your benefit, the sweat running down those handsome faces, those erect phalluses swaying back and forth - all for your benefit. It's a heady experience, Guilo," John padded me on the back. "Thanks for opening our eyes to a new use for slavemeat - you've shown us there's a lot more to slaves than just a body waiting your table and some fresh meat for your bed."

The other six guests clamored to go next, but quickly reconciled themselves to waiting their turn, two by two. By the time the fourth trip was completed and all eight guests had been given an initial ride - all the same distance at the same pace - the eight slaves powering the litter were no longer panting, but gasping; the sweat running down their bodies were now riverlets, and their left or right tits, dependent on which side they were positioned, were red and swollen from the constant pulling of the leashes. Their swollen penises were now coated with pre-cum, as the muscles of their shoulders, rumps, and legs quivered in fatigue from the heavy loads

All eight guests were as enthusiastic as John Morgan and, after completing their demonstration ride, went on and on about the sheer ecstasy they felt as the slaves labored beneath them; the feeling of power and control the litter ride gave them, and the erotic display the slaves and the litter made, especially when it was in action with the slaves gasping and sweating from the forced pace and the heavy loads imposed on their bodies. All thanked their host profusely for sharing this experience with them and if was obvious, most of them were already planning such a conveyance for themselves as soon as the right type of slaves could be located, purchased, and trained appropriately. There were a thousand questions directed at me as to best size of slave; the training involved the endurance of the slaves, and on and on. It was obvious not all questions could be answered right now, so I suggested we discuss this at a leisurely dinner I had arranged to be served in the main dining room where these very litter slaves, freshly cleaned inside and out, would be waiting on them throughout the dinner, and - I winked suggestively - after we've through supping.

"Can we bring our own slaves if we want?" John Morgan asked and several other guests looked concerned.

"Of course, John," I replied, "as long as they too are completely cleansed inside and out, are as naked as my own slaves will be, and have all been lubricated for the 'fun' things we all enjoy doing."

This brought a lot of laughter from everyone and we retired to the lounge outside the dining room where Sergei fixed everyone drinks while we waited for the litter slaves to be delivered, fresh and ready for the events of the rest of the afternoon and evening.

Sergei served drinks all around, checked for refills, and, after that disappeared. Within a half hour, however, he was back again, this time with 22 freshly scrubbed slaves, all collared, many tit-ringed, and, of course, eight of them genitally banded.

The slaves the guests had brought were highly varied. Some were black, some brown, some yellow, some white. They were all sizes and shapes - everything from young 18-year-old boys just beginning to reach maturity and weighing no more than 120 pounds to burly slaves in their early 30s that would top a scale at close to 250 pounds. Three were tit-ringed, only one had his equipment banded, four had ear rings permanently installed, and two sported nose rings that seemed to be welded shut. All were heavily collared, all seemed to accept their slavery without question at this point, and all were obviously used to being naked most of the time. Most of them were heavily hung for their size and the majority were already sporting semi-erections. Balls ranged from small to large, and most hung down between their legs rather alarmingly, as if they'd been stretched somewhere along the line. It was a look I didn't particularly care for, and I was glad my own slaves were all banded to prevent such a thing. A few had magnificent physiques but most were well-built but not exceptional. Most were body shaved - those that weren't either didn't have much natural body hair or their owners obviously bought them for their animal-like hairy appearance. Indeed, one was so hairy he looked like the missing link to me, but his owner must have been turned on by it for some reason or another.

My litter bearers served the meal as they'd been trained to do by Sergei, their magnificent physiques shining with a fresh coat of oil as they did so. The visiting slaves served their masters individually as directed - everything from cutting their food into small bits for them, milking themselves to produce a good supply of condiment their master enjoyed with his meal, or slipping under the table to suck their masters off as they enjoyed their meal. Some knelt close by as their masters played with their tits, stuck their fingers up their upended holes, stroked their rampant pricks, massaged their balls, or wiped their greasy hands off in their slave's hair in lieu of the provided napkin. It was obvious all of these slaves were acclimated to such service and none of them seemed to be humiliated in the slightest at these requests.

As the meal leisurely progressed, all of the questions got answered about how they too could fit themselves out with a litter and team, the training involved, and what it would cost, figuring in the initial cost of the stock plus training and maintenance. Since the diners frequently interrupted their meal for some dalliance with their own slaves, by the time they got around to the dessert course, five hours or more had elapsed.

I had gotten so exasperated at the pace of the meal, I too followed their lead and had Sergei suck me off under the table at one point. But it gave my own litter bearers a good chance to rest up and study the other slaves in action. Most of my slave boys were fascinated by the nose rings installed in two of the slaves and wondered what use those rings were put to in the slave's lives. I saw some of them rubbing the tissue between their nostrils as if they were trying to imagine being fitted with a nose ring. Even while serving the meal, and despite the wide availability of all the other slaves, my eight got their bodies fondled frequently, their shafts stoked, their balls weighed, and their tit-rings played with every time they bent over the table to serve another course - actions they endured willingly enough, although some of them seemed rather stoic about it. They knew full well they would be placed at the total disposal of the guests the minute the meal was over and were glad they had the chance to rest up before they were ordered into full compliance with whatever these guests desired.

As soon as the meal had been cleared away, my eight litter slaves were ordered to full display in the dining hall

"We're going to play a little game. I going to ask a question connected with this slave meat you see displayed in front of you. The first one to guess the correct answer will get that slave for his evening's entertainment. Of course, when you're finished with them, you might want to share them with the other guests, or perhaps trade around a bit," I winked as they all laughed.

"The first question is," I paused dramatically, "which of these slaves comes from a country where the capitol is Kiev?"

A guest from the United States quickly pointed at the Ukrainian slave.

"Correct, Bruce. He's all yours for the evening," as Sergei, whip in hand, lead the selected slave over to the winning guest where, under Sergei's commands, he quickly knelt and kissed the feet of his 'master for the evening.'

Everyone clapped for the winner and made ribald suggestions as to how best to use the slave.

"Next question," I again paused dramatically once I had their attention. "Which slave comes from a country that rhymes with 'had'?"

There was a long pause of several minutes as the guests mulled the question over and mumbled among themselves. Finally, a Frenchmen pointed to the black from Chad exclaiming, "I should have recognized a slave from one of our former colonies."

Everyone clapped as Sergei gripped the erect prick of the black and, using that as a handle, led the slave over to the Frenchman's seat where he was directed to prostrate himself before his new 'master' in total obeisance.

Next question: "Which property in front of you has seen the Southern Cross?"

Again there was a long pause as each of the slaves on display felt the guests' eyes pouring over them. Finally, one pointed to the Australian slave.

"Correct," I announced, "the Aussie is all yours for the night," as applause greeted my announcement.

This time, Sergei stuck the handle of his whip up the asshole of the Aussie and pushed/led the slave boy to the winner, an older German, where he was told to kneel with his lips on the floor as Sergei pumped the whip handle in and out a few times to establish the mood.

"Next question," I continued. "Which piece of meat displayed here tonight had ancestors that worshiped volcanos?"

Instantly, several guest pointed at the Polynesian slave.

"I think you were first," I said, pointing to another German guest.

Sergei put his finger through the Polynesian slave's tit ring and led him to the German, motioning for the new German master to put his own finger where Sergei's currently was as a "transfer of ownership" for the evening.

All that was left standing after a while was the Chinese slave and the only guest without a slave assigned to him was John Morgan.

I turned to John and asked, "Which slave loves to have his big juicy tits played with and could be described as a 'tit freak' in that he shoots off every time his tits are properly stimulated?"

A huge smile went across John's face. "How thoughtful of you, Guilo," as Sergei fastened a chain connecting both tit rings and then, gapping the chain, pulled the Chinese slave over to Mr. Morgan, placing the chain in his hand as he stretched the Chinese slave's tits a good inch away from his massive pecs in the process.

"Oh," moaned the Chinese slave as his tits were stretched and pre-cum started dripping out of his erect prick.

"Look at the bastard, Guilo," John said delightedly. "He's about to shoot already."

From that point on, the guests' own slaves got time off for the main part. The litter slaves were put to instant use and, within the hour, most of them had already been fucked thoroughly, had sucked their new "masters" off at least once, and had every part of their body fingered and fondled. By the second hour, they were being traded around among the guests who demanded a whole new round of sexual services. By the third hour, most of the guests were totally drained and amused themselves by having the slaves fuck each other, suck each other off, or fucking the slaves they had brought with them or having their own slaves suck the litter slaves off. By the sixth hour, all the slaves as well as all their masters didn't have a drop left in them and most were falling asleep wherever they could lay down.

Finally, even Sergei had been drained dry and the only two people awake were John Morgan and myself.

"Guilo," John Morgan whispered. "I've got a little treat for you."

"Really?" I replied. "What is it?"

"It's out in the back of my SUV. Let's get some fresh air and I'll show you."

Both of us more or less dragged ourselves away from the dining room, now reeking with the heavy smell of oozing hot lubricant, drying cum on most of the slave's bodies, tons of raw body sweat, and drooling saliva.

John Morgan took me out to the parking area, reached into the back seat of his SUV to extract a slave whip, and then proceeded to unlock the tail gate. Inside was a shiny metal shipping cage and inside that was crammed a naked body, fully restrained with his wrists shackled to his neck collar and his ankles hobbled together with a close 8" chain. John unlocked the cage, and, smacking the whip hard over the exposed rump, ordered the slave out of the cage.

The slave howled from the pain of the whip as he quickly shuffled out of the cage as best he could with all the restraints on him to avoid yet another blow of the sharp-edged whip. As he emerged, I saw his nose had been ringed between the two nostrils and both tits had been pierced with the thickest rings I'd ever seen - both the nose and tit rings were a good half-inch in diameter. He had not been body shaved and his hairy body, covered in bristly black hair, gave him a distinctive 'animal' appearance.

"Stand up, you bastard," John Morgan commanded as his whip wrapped around the hairy body once again, drawing a little blood on the slave's back. The slave screamed in pain and a frantic look of panic filled his eyes, tears spilling down his cheeks as the scream turned into a series of sobs.

"What... what... is it?" I asked, startled by the slave's wild stare.

"It's a slave freshly taken... A wild bastard... A slave with no training whatsoever under his sorry skin yet. He's a Brit construction worker that got himself too drunk a couple of nights ago and one of England's notorious slave catchers got him. Those guys sell their stock as soon as they can in that they like to get rid of their catches as soon as they can to avoid feeding them, they say. I say it's because they are scared to death of getting caught in the act," John laughed. "Anyway, I bought him night before last, not four hours after he'd been caught and had them tit and nose ring him while he was still dead drunk. When the bastard woke up finally, I had the collar on him, his wrists fastened to the collar and his ankles shackled just like you see him now. He had no idea of where he was or what had happened, other than his nose septum hurt like hell and his tits were inflamed and burnt like fire. Thank God I had him caged because he tried everything in the book to get loose - didn't do him a bit of good, of course.

"I've never seen a slave that wasn't broken to slavery pretty well," I commented. "This one's as rogue as they get, looks like."

"Yes, rogue is a good word for it, Guilo. This poor son of a bitch has no family, so he won't be missed, but he was so naive he didn't know there were still slaves in the world, he didn't have a clue that slaves were used sexually, and he'd obviously never heard of, let alone see up close, locked slave collars, nose and tit rings, and cages for human stock. His whole world is brand new to him. Look at that look of panic on the bastard's face, Guilo. It's going to take months to break this boy I tell you."

"At least," was all I could say. "Maybe a lot longer. I hope you didn't pay much for him as I reached forward to grab his balls, but he lurched back as far as could within the limitations of his shackled feet before John let fly with the whip again and again, each stroke wrapping itself clear around the torso of the new slave before revealing the new open weals laid upon his hide. The slave screamed anew as he bent over, trying to avoid the slave whip cutting into his skin.

"Stand up straight there, slave, and get those legs apart as best you can. The master here wants to examine your balls."

"No...no..." the slave wailed, as a fresh barrage of blows descended on his body.

"Very well," John said calmly as he continued to beat the slave fiercely. "We'll just have to put that new nose ring to some use," he announced as he quickly grabbed the nose ring and jerked it until the slave's head was drawn all the way back, a fresh scream of raw pain emanating from the slave as the ring dug into the still unhealed incisions in his nose septum and a flesh flow of blood began oozing out of his nose.

"Now, slave boy, you'll pay attention," John announced as he jerked the nose ring forward and twisted it a little, jerking the slave into an upright position as the boy screamed again and turned pale from the severe pain.

"Now you can feel his balls, Guilo, can't he, slaveboy?" John said calmly, keeping a steady tension on the distended nose ring.

When the slave didn't respond, John gave another vicious tug on the ring, and with his other hand twisted one of the slave's tit rings a full 90 degrees. The slave gasped in renewed pain and gasped out another wrenching scream.

"Can't he, slaveboy?" John repeated, again twisting the rings as hard as he could.

"Yes...yes..." the slave gasped.

"Yes, what, slave?" John twisted the rings even harder.

"Yes... yes... sir?" the slave moaned, too week with pain to scream any longer.

"There... that's better," John said, pulling but not twisting the rings in his hands.

"Guilo, he's all ready for you to feel his balls now," John prompted, never letting lose of the rings.

I reached forward and hefted the slave's amble balls. They felt strange with hair all over them - I personally liked them smooth skinned - but, when I squeezed them firmly, they were so full I was sure John hadn't allowed the slave to empty them since he had been captured. A low moan was the slave's only response to my ball squeezing.

"If you don't mind, Guilo, stroke the slave until he's good and hard," John said. "I don't want to use him if he's not all hot and bothered," he laughed.

"John, how in the hell can you fuck an animal that's wild?" I asked in amazement. "He'll kill you if he ever gets loose."

"That's what the nose ring is for. See that snap hook I've installed on the floor of the SUV. I'll just lock his nose ring to that hook and with his wrists shackled to his collar, there's not a damn thing he can do when I fuck him but wiggle and scream," John laughed as he quickly locked the slave's nose ring to the embedded hook which resulted in the slave's ass positioned just right for a good fucking with his shackled feet supporting his weight firmly on the ground.

"Ever fucked an untrained slave?" John said. "It's an experience you'll never forget. That's my little treat for you, Guilo. He's all yours."

"No, I haven't," I admitted, "and now that he seems secure, it might be novel," I admitted as I opened the robe I had grabbed to wear outside and began stroking myself a little in readiness. "Is he lubed, John?" I asked.

"No... Makes it all the better, Guilo. Go ahead, poke him... You'll love the way he screams when you feed it to him."

I felt almost savage but couldn't resist the novelty of it all. I positioned myself behind the twitching, struggling slave, closely bound by the highly restricting nose ring and both hands clamped to his neck collar, reached around and grabbed his sore, swollen tits to better control him, and drove up his tight hole inch by inch.

The slave tried to clamp his hole shut, but my continued pressure soon overcame that, and as my shaft worked its way up his dry virginal canal, he bucked violently as he screamed at the top of his lungs.

"You son of a bitch," he yelled, "you God damn son of a bitch, you fucking bastard, you damn perverted bastard," he screamed as I drove all the way in. "I'll kill you, you bastard," he moaned as I began pumping him steadily, appreciating the feelings the contractions of his anal muscles gave my shaft.

"The boy's a real virgin - about as tight as they get," I laughed as I increased the tempo. "Haven't you fucked him yourself John?" The slave continued to buck as he screamed out his threats and curses.

"Only two or three times so far," John said. "Certainly not enough to open him up at all. Don't you love that raw resistance - that total revulsion to what is happening to him - the agony he seems to be putting himself through as he's completely and totally raped. He's so totally humiliated - so shamed - so repulsed by what's happening - it's really a totally different experience from using a well trained slave like we generally have available."

I drove even deeper into the slave's hole and continued to play with his raw, sensitized tits which only increased the slave's agony.

"I grant you it's different alright, John. I don't think it's the best fuck I've ever had, but you do get a rush of power that's intoxicating that you don't get with most slaves you fuck who are surprised if you don't fuck them at every opportunity. In fact, most of mine are so trained by now they love to be fucked anyway you want to do it."

"Exactly," John replied. "That gets boring after a while. Once in a while, I like to fuck a boy who fights you every inch of the way. I can almost feel their deep shame - the humiliation to the core of their macho self - the fact they have no idea yet their body is simply a owned piece of meat. They still think it's their body, not ours. It's real novel and, as you say, there is a power rush in it - you really understand what power a master has when you actually rape someone instead of just using them."

Within minutes, despite all the activity I'd already had that day, I once again felt myself getting ready to shoot and, pushing even deeper into the slave's ass, shot what little cum I had left deep into his anal cavity.

When the slave realized I had shot, he again cursed me and shivered in repulsion, knowing he was now carrying my seed within his body. As I withdrew, my prick was coated in cum, shit, and blood.

"Sorry, Guilo," John said as he handed me a rag to clean myself. "I could possibly force this bastard to clean you with his mouth, but I'd be scared he'd bite you. Too risky at this point, I'm afraid, nose ring or not!" he laughed.

"Are you going to fuck him now?" I asked.

"I think I will, as long as I've gone to all this trouble," he answered. Without further ado, he stripped down and promptly shoved his full length into the bleeding hole of the slave who screamed anew, knowing his torment was far from over. John proceeded to fuck the slave vigorously which took some time since John had been drained dry by his antics in the dining room. Finally, he summoned up a small amount out of his drained balls which eventually, with a lot of pumping and stroking, exploded into the slave's bruised hole.

By this time, the slave's nose was bleeding profusely since the nose ring he had been fastened by had been yanked and tugged many times during both his fuckings.

When John withdrew, there was even more blood on his prick than there had been on mine and I handed him the rag to clean himself as the slave was reduced to uttering a few curses under his breathe and groaning in agony from his ravished hole, the whip bites on his body, his swollen, bleeding tits, and his raw nose septum also bleeding profusely now.

"What are you going to do with him?" I asked.

"Put him back in his cage, Guilo. Did you want him up at the house?"

"No, no, John. I meant what are you going to do with a raw rogue slave like that once you get him home and he heals up?"

"I haven't decided yet, Guilo. I bought him dirt cheap as you can imagine so I haven't too much invested in him at this point. I could sell him off to a good training school who will then eventually market him, or I could try to train the bastard myself."

By this time, John had unlatched the nose ring from the embedded hook and with a volley of whip lashes, drove the slave back into his cage which was quickly locked. As the slave scooted around in the cage so he could see out, he managed to spit at his master which infuriated John. He promptly reached through the bars, grabbed the nose ring and locked it to one of the bars with a padlock he kept handy.

"There, you bastard," John said as he wiped the spit off his face. "You'll think twice about spitting at your master again after being ringed like that bouncing around back here. Besides," he smiled, "there's no way you can do anything now but keep your face pressed against the bars. That will be your only rest," he smiled as he reached through again and twisted the nose ring painfully. The slave screamed from the depths of his being which seemed to satisfy John for the moment.

"If it were me, I'll sell him to Guiliano Imports for anything they would give me. They've got a trainer at their Greek facility - one of their slaves named Santos - who is a real marvel. In about 15 months or so under his tutelage, this brute could be one of those slave boys serving us so well at dinner tonight. If you're really interested in him, you could always buy him back from Guiliano, once he was properly trained.

"Fifteen months?" John exclaimed. "Is that how long it takes to fully break a slave?"

"That's what they told me at Guiliano when I bought my litter slaves. It's a lot shorter if they were born into slavery or they had been a slave for years before, but a slave that was free before - 15 months to fully break them. They ought to know, John. They're in the business."

"Well, that settles it, then, Guilo. I don't have the patience or time to fiddle around for 15 months with this worthless piece of shit. If I were doing the training, he'd probably be dead in two weeks because I'll beat the last breath out of him. Imagine - spitting on his master! I should just beat him to death now and make us both feel better about it. But... you know, Guilo, I'm too tight. I'm sure Guiliano Imports will pay me more for this sorry mass of muscle than the trifling I paid the slave catcher for him. Then they can have this Santos, or whatever his name is, beat, burn, and fuck the bastard for 15 months or whatever it takes to make him worth something on the open market. I'll call them on my way back to the airport and arrange for them to pick the sorry bastard up for shipping down to their training facility. Meanwhile, I'm not going to feed or water him and, once I get him out of my car, I'm not going to allow toilet privileges, so the bastard can just lie in his own shit caged up the entire time until they take possession. Serves him right and maybe that will teach him he's not calling the shots anymore."

"A good plan, John," I counseled. "I have a feeling you would kill him with your whip in no time at all. This way you'll probably end up making a little off of him -Guiliano Imports will give you a decent price even though he is about as rogue as they've probably encountered. Nevertheless, I have a feeling that their Santos will simply see it as a challenge and have him broken and totally compliant in a year or so. Meanwhile, thanks for the experience, John. It was unique, to say the least. But I'm sticking with trained slaves myself. It's considerably more pleasant - power trip or not!"

"Me too," John admitted. "These wild stock just aren't worth the trouble of feeding them."

With that, both of them headed back to the manor house for a well deserved rest.

When Sergei woke up, everyone was sound asleep, not surprising in view of all the activities just four or five hours ago, he thought. He was glad to see his master and his friend John Morgan were deep in sleep on one of the sofas. Rising silently, he went to each of the slaves and with a finger to his lips to indicate they should be totally quiet, he rounded all 22 of them up and had them silently move back to the slave quarters where he would supervise their showers, their enemas, their body shaves (for those already body shaved), and their breakfast. He decided not to milk the eight litter slaves who had been totally drained just hours before nor did he feel he had the right to milk slaves not belonging to his master. If the master wanted his morning cocktail, he could always order it delivered when he had breakfast, whenever that might be. That way it would be warm and fresh.

The communal shower and cleansing rituals gave the slaves a chance to meet each other and compare their circumstances - a rare privilege for most slaves owned by single masters - a privilege Sergei knew they would appreciate and which he himself was interested in.

Initially, most of the questions from the visiting slaves were directed toward the litter slaves about where they were bought, their training on the litter, how much and how often they got fed, how many hours a day did they get to sleep, were the slave quarters always this clean and sweet smelling, whether the tit rings bothered them very much, how did it feel to have their genitals banded continually, how often they got fucked by the master and his steward, how often they had to entertain guests like today, whether their master let them play with each other if he wasn't using them, and whether their master had a stud farm, and, if so, how often they were put to stud there. Most were brazen enough to ask how much their master had paid for them, usually comparing that price with what they had sold for at their last sale.

Sergei listened carefully to all the questions and the quickly forthcoming answers from the slaves under his supervision, reminding himself that those treated like animals quickly become like animals - animals that were easy to manage. None of the litter slaves found the questions unusual, almost as if they expected nothing less when interrogated by other slaves, and poured forth elaborate answers. All took great pride in telling how they were milked every morning so their balls got drained regularly, a fact received with awe and enthusiasm by the visiting slaves who reluctantly admitted they often had to go weeks and weeks before they got relief of some sort. The litter slave's pride in their purchase price bordered on arrogance but slaves have their pride too, Sergei reminded himself, thinking of his own purchase price years ago and how proud he had been at the time to think he was worth that much to a master.

Then it was the turn of the litter slaves to ask questions of the visitors. What did they do other than satisfy their masters sexually? Where were they trained? How long did their training last? How long after they were trained until someone bought them? How many masters had they had? How much did they bring at their last sale? How often did they get fucked every day or have to suck someone off? Did they ever wear clothes? Did they see free people other than their masters often? Did they think their masters would sell them in the near future? If so, would they probably be sold to a company or another individual master like they had now? Had any of them been owned by a mistress? If so, how did she use them and how often? Had any of them served stud at a breeding facility or with their master's females slaves? Had any of them ever worked in a male brothel? If so, did they like it? How often did they get to shoot off? Did they get enough food? Was the food tasty or was it just standard slave chow? Did they get to piss and shit when they needed to or did they have to have their master's permission first? Were there cages clean? (When three of them announced they weren't caged at night, the others asked where they slept - all three slept chained to their master's bed it turned out.) How many hours a day did they have to exercise or did their work assignments keep their bodies in shape? And, for the few that weren't body shaved, why did their masters want all that hair on them? How often did they get loaned out to their master's friends and business partners? For the three fitted with nose rings, they asked what it felt like, why they had been fitted with nose rings to start with, and how long, if ever, did it take to get use to them?

Sergei analyzed both the questions and the answers to ascertain the success of his stewardship of the slaves. He came to the quick conclusion his master's slaves were content, even happy in their own slavery, that they felt their treatment was exceptional considering they were just owned property, and that they weren't asked to do anything a slave shouldn't expect to be asked to do anytime, anywhere. None of them seemed to want to trade places with the visiting slaves - their lives were no better than their own - and, sometimes, judging from some of the questions they were asking - they obviously considered some visiting slave's had things somewhat more demanding than what they were used to. Of course, Sergei thought, most of the visiting slaves hadn't cost as much as the litter slaves, so what did you expect? Slaves got treated pretty much according to their value on the auction block. Look at all the cheap ugly slaves bought up by corporations for working in the mines, construction crews, and assembly line work hidden away throughout the world. They didn't cost much to start with and their treatment reflected it - worked beyond endurance under a heavy whip or electric prod to an early grave, fed garbage and slop, never allowed enough sleep, and never given any opportunity to relieve their sex needs. All of these slaves discussing their pampered lives, Sergei reflected, were young, exceptionally good looking, well hung, well built, and sexually appealing. They were the lucky ones when it came to slavery - much like himself, happily. He's always been privileged in his slavery and he knew it. Thank God he'd been born, like those around him now, with a beautiful face, a magnificent body, and big, easy to arouse sexual equipment. All it took other than that to get decent care was a willing attitude, an eager-to-please compliance with a master's desires, and an air of absolute obedience that delighted any buyer.

When the cleansing and the chatter was finished, Sergei took his whip and quietly marched the freshened slaves back to their masters, still asleep in the manor. He told the slaves to keep absolutely quiet, sitting over in a corner, until they saw their master's awaken. At that point, they were to quickly crawl over to their master and kneel beside him, awaiting his orders. Most, he pointed out, would probably enjoy a good sucking upon awakening. Others might want to drain their slave's balls as a liquid breakfast. He doubted if many wanted to fuck them this early after last night, a comment that brought a few quietly muted chuckles from the slaves. All the slaves smiled at Sergei, appreciating his obvious great supervisory skills with slaves. But the visiting slaves were especially appreciative of him, knowing he guided them smoothly through all that was expected of them in this new environment. The few Sergei had explored sexually for his own enjoyment didn't mind - it certainly was his privilege as their overseer and use of their body was the least they could do for an overseer so through - as well as thoughtful - making sure they were fed, cleaned, and even allowed to talk to the other slaves. The whole visit, even if this was the end of it, was a rare threat for them, in large part due to Sergei.

As the masters woke up one by one, Sergei had predicted it right. Some wanted to be sucked immediately, some wanted a morning cocktail out of their slave's loins, but the majority were totally worn out from last night and were satiated with the slave's willing bodies by that point. Instead, they wanted their coffee, some eggs and pancakes, and fresh orange juice, which Sergei had once again anticipated and had all ready for the slaves to serve their masters.

By mid morning, most of the masters were snapping leashes onto the collars of the slaves that would be returning in the boot or caged in the back of an SUV, watching the slaves driving them don their carefully folded clothes, and, before long, all were gone except

Sergei, the eight litter slaves now thoroughly cleaning the entire manor house under Sergei's ever-present whip and me.

The visit had been fun. I had been able to show off my new contraption, including my well trained litter slaves, and renew old acquaintances. I planned to do it again sometime.

That afternoon, I took a prolonged ride in the litter - we went at a mild trot - and covered almost every road and trail on the estate's grounds. By the time we returned, Sergei was patiently waiting, as usual, to unleash their tit rings from the rails, get the litter put away, and get the slaves cleaned inside and out for the evening. The slaves were pretty well exhausted, panting heavily with almost all the sweat completely worked out of them by this time. Their tits were flame red and swollen from the irritation of the swinging leashes. But they were obviously a happy lot. Every single one of those pieces of beautiful slave flesh sported a full dripping erection, every single one had a smile on his face, and each was grateful I had ordered the milking to resume in the morning. Their appreciation at that announcement was evident in their grateful eyes as they all gave me a look of pure appreciation - even love?

I asked Sergei that night if slaves ever loved their owners.

"Of course, master," Sergei responded without hesitation. "Haven't you noticed my love for you?"

"But why, Sergei? After all, we own your bodies - we control your lives?"

"Yes. That accounts for part of our love for our owners, master. You are the source of fulfilling all our needs - our food, our health, even our sex outlets. How could we not love you?"

When I looked skeptical, Sergei added, "It's not bullshit, master. Look at it this way. Everyone wants to love, even slaves. What else do slaves have to love but our master? We don't have families; we don't have mates; we don't have children that we live with even if we are being put to stud; we no longer have a mother or father. Our master is all of those."

"Yes, Sergei. I see your point. You probably do love your masters in some strange way for those reasons. But we do own you body and soul. You're just property we can sell at any time we want to anyone we choose."

"Of course, master. That is the privilege of any owner, master. But, master, everyone wants to belong to something or someone -

slaves are human even if they are property. Free people belong to their own families, their professions, their educational backgrounds and social status, their wealth, their spouses, their nation - I could go on and on. Slaves have none of those things available to belong to - so we belong to our master or mistress. It's a big part of a slave's need - to belong to whatever they can, and in a slave's case the only option is to belong to someone else. Masters fill a real need within us, master, and, to us, that's a good reason to love our masters. If we don't, master, we have nothing and lose everything - we're like those draft slaves you see with nothing in their eyes and only move when a whip bits into their back. I don't expect you to understand my rambling, master. I never understood this until I was well into my own slavery and had finally accepted it - only then did I learn to unrequitedly love my master."

"I bought a slave and got a psychoanalyst," I laughed. "But what you say makes sense somehow. I suppose if I were a slave I'd agree with you. At any rate," I laughed again, "my new litter slaves seem to buy it. They seem to love you, Sergei, for all the wrong reasons as best I can figure out. You beat them, you cage them, you give them enemas, you fuck them, you have them suck you off, you milk them each morning, you work them hard around the clock, and you withdraw their food and water if they don't please you in every way. Yet they seem to love you for it."

"And they love you, master, for buying them and putting them to some use."

"Well, that I can understand, Sergei."

PART II

John Morgan watched the former British construction worker whimpering in his cage, his back and rump laced with the bright red weals of a recent whipping, his nose still bleeding by the fact his large nose ring was very tightly attached to the cage's bars, rendering him effectively immobile. Both shackled wrists were attached to his thick, tall metal collar which forced his head into an upright position. His ankles were shackled together, so any movement within the tiny cage was impossible. His long, thick penis, neatly circumcised and well-shaped, drooped over his large ball sac. A thick penis gag was forced down his throat, held in place by a series of straps around his head, making speech of any type impossible. Lastly, a thick butt plug had been forced up his tender, inflamed ass chute, still sore and smarting after his series of rapes a week or so ago. The latter appliance also kept him from soiling his cage, a nasty problem on his recent trip from some other man's private villa in Italy back to his present circumstances God knew where. His hairy body was still wet from the recent high-pressure hosing he'd received when he was transferred from his shipping cage to the heavy duty cage he was in now. That hosing had cut the stench and washed away all the residual of being caged 72 hours with no facilities, but had been quickly followed by the huge plug being forced up his rear which made him feel as if he were being split in half.

"Got the bastard back to England fine," John Morgan, the English billionaire reported on his cell phone to Guilo Parsimi, the Italian friend he had recently visited. "He's none the worse for wear and even seems to be calming down a bit, especially now that he's fitted with both a penis gag and a butt plug. I'd brand the SOB good and proper if I didn't plan to sell him off - a good branding usually does wonders to teach a new slave his place in the world."

The caged slave, hearing this announcement, trembled in raw fear and would have thrown up in panic if his penis gag would have allowed such a response. His eyes drew wide in fear and then tears began flowing once again.

"I take it you're going to follow my advice and sell the rogue slave, then," Guilo responded. "To Guiliano Imports down off the Greek coast as I suggested, or to one of your local dealers there in England?"

"Well, not exactly sell him, Guilo. I've decided to trade him in for some decently trained stock. Your Guiliano Import stock appeared to be well trained and I doubt if your in-house overseer, Sergei, is responsible for all of that - he probably just honed the slaves to your particular preferences and maintained the training they'd already received," John Morgan reported. "You won't believe it, Guilo, but I'm down to just four slaves now not including that wild bastard I drug all the way over to your place in Italy to show you. It takes more than four to keep this estate going no matter how much they're disciplined - there's just too much to do, especially if I want them fresh for my bed when I'm in the mood."

"I suppose you also expect them to entertain your guests?" Guilo added. "I know my own slaves spend more time than you would think just doing that."

"Of course," John Morgan replied. "That alone keeps them pretty well drained. On certain weeks, it seems like this is an airline terminal there are so damn many guests here, all expecting a receptive ass or a warm mouth at their disposal around the clock," he chuckled.

"Well, I'm sure your guests have plenty of slaves at home and so they can hardly be expected to go without for very long," Guilo laughed. "I know when I visit, I've always kept a handsome slave or two of yours pretty busy."

"Pretty busy is British understatement if I've ever heard it," John laughed. "More like they're so sore and overused by the time you leave, it takes them four or five days to recover," he chortled.

"Well, how many new ones are you planning to buy?" Guilo got back to the topic at hand.

"I was thinking of six - all matched for size and color," John shot back.

"Sounds like some interesting new project, John," Guilo queried.

"It is, Guilo," John said. "I hired an engineer to design it for me. He calls it a SPV for slave powered vehicle, but whatever you call it, it's damn ingenious. Doesn't have the baroque style of your litter, but it's more high tech."

"High tech?" Guilo asked, definitely curious now.

"Yes, Guilo. The front looks like a deluxe golf cart for up to four persons with the steering and brake controls just like a golf cart. But the back of it, completely open so you can view what's going on, houses two rows of three slaves, each row fastened to their own treadmill that provides all the power. Each slave is fastened by his neck collar, tit rings and his genital band to the contraption so he has to hold his position at all times. He's also fitted with a wireless electronic butt plug and another wireless device hooked to his collar that's programmed into the accelerator and brake. The more you push down on the accelerator, the more of a jolt goes up their ass; the harder you press the brake, the more juice flies into their neck collar. It's programmed just short of tissue damage, but it can be mighty painful, they tell me, if you drive them hard. Works like a charm - at least in the preliminary tests - and gets the last ounce of energy out of the slaves hooked up to it. When you've got the accelerator down at least half way, their feet are flying on those treadmills and the sweat is rolling off the slaves' bodies as they struggle to suck in enough oxygen to keep them going at that pace. When you see if in action, it makes for a nice display, especially if you've got some really good looking slaves being displayed in the engine compartment."

"I could see where it would make the usual battery powered golf carts seem prosaic by comparison," Guilo said with obvious admiration. "In my opinion, as you know from my litter, muscular slaves, panting and sweating profusely in their assignments, always make for a good display, especially if they're good looking specimens to start with. You're going to display them naked, aren't you, John?"

"Of course, Guilo. Even we Britishers aren't priggish enough to try to cover our slaves anymore, especially the well built, well hung boys I intend to buy. Imagine that litter of yours without the naked slaves chained by their tits to it and their erect sex thrust out for all to see with those genital bands welded on them. Wouldn't be effective at all if they even had a tiny loincloth to cover themselves. Otherwise, it would be as boring as, well, the Roman litters you used for inspiration."

"Whose to say what the Romans really did with their litter slaves?" Guilo asked. "I imagine the truth has been censured by all those pious little monks recopying the material in the Middle Ages. My guess is that the Romans' litter bearers probably looked more like mine than they do in all the pictures you see in encyclopedias and in Hollywood movies. The Romans were hardly known for being Victorian, you know, Guilo chuckled. "After all, they were my ancestors so I should know - their needs as a master would be no different than mine today. Masters aren't any different today than they were then and we know slaves aren't, once they're trained."

"Well, my golf cart sure makes a statement and it is fun to drive," John Morgan said.

"It's going to cost you some real money to make that momma run," Guilo laughed. "Your trade-in isn't going to make a dent in what that's going to cost."

"Probably not, but I'm rid of the bastard at least and he can start being trained properly for his new life. Maybe someday I'll buy him back - he's a mighty fine piece of meat actually, especially if you got all that hair off of him, but it's going to take at least two years of solid training in my opinion - no matter how good this Guiliano Imports is in breaking a rogue slave."

The slave being discussed broke into a fresh round of tears as he felt the bile in his stomach again try to get past the thick penis gag rammed down his throat.

"What color?" Guilo asked.

"What color what?" John shot back.

"You said your team was going to be matched, so what color did you want them?" Guilo said, impatiently.

"Oh, that. I was thinking of milk-chocolate brown. I've always liked black blood in my slaves, but I think the milk-chocolate coloring makes the most attractive. At least, those are the ones I especially like to bed down."

"They are good looking generally," Guilo conceded. "At least the ones with the great physiques and who are well hung which is the only type you'd pick out anyway," Guilo laughed. "But it's hard to match to the exact same color - you're going to have to pay extra, I bet, to get six of them the same shade and still be well built and well hung."

"Probably, Guilo, but brown skinned slaves are still sort of a novelty here in England and I think my guests would like to try out a black slave given the opportunity. They're probably sick to death of all the white blonds that have flooded the market since the Eastern European supplies became available."

"What are Italian slaves bringing at your auctions now?" Guilo asked.

"Still near the top bids," John Morgan answered, "if they're real good looking, nicely built, and decently equipped. You do come from a good looking race of people, Guilo." John laughed. "And how are the English slaves selling at your auctions?"

"Blue-eyed ones are selling fairly well, but, overall, I'd say about mid-range. Blacks, mulattos, Americans, Italians, Germans, Australian, Canadian and Polynesians are top bids, all things being equal. The English, Irish, French, Spaniards, Poles, and Russians are about mid-range. South and Central Americans, Mexicans, Indians, any of the Balkans and Middle Eastern countries and almost all Asians are dirt cheap - they've simply flooded the market with so many it's hard to get much for them anymore. That why, John, Guiliano Imports, or any other reputable dealer, is going to ask plenty for matched blacks who are perfectly trained."

"I know," John said, "but I'm used to getting what I want."

"Well, John, you can afford to do just that. I wanted a team of eight matched slaves of different colors. I got just what I wanted, but it wasn't cheap."

"Guilo, you're hardly starving to death yourself. That villa of yours puts my estate to shame although here in England the place turns heads. But I do need to spruce it up with some interesting stock. Guilo, with six more slaves on hand, I'm going to need an overseer as well. You couldn't be persuaded to sell me that Sergei of yours, could you?"

"As you astutely observed, Sergei has proven to be an excellent slave overseer. John, I've owned Sergei for years and years, but he's getting along and occasionally I've thought of selling him. He'd be perfect for your needs. Tell you what, John. There's an overseer called Santos owned by Guiliano Imports. He's about as appealing and good looking as any man ever gets on this earth. You buy him, loan him to me for the duration, and I'll loan you Sergei to get your bevy of slaves organized. The change of pace would do him good, you love to fuck Sergei if I recall correctly, and by the time you've about worn him out, we'll trade back. You can take your property Santos and I'll get back Sergei. Santos is Italian and will enjoy a visit back to his country of origin. Sergei has never been to England and the trip would do him good, but he is the best there is when it comes to managing slaves like you're planning to buy as well as shaping up the ones you have on hand. John, if you really enjoy Sergei in bed, as I suspect you will indefinitely, I'll consider transferring his ownership papers over to you as long as you let me keep this slave Santos I've got the hots for."

"I've never laid eyes on this Santos, but he must be something," John chortled. "I'm assuming you're at least going to let me fuck him a few times before I bring him to your villa to pick up Sergei just to see what all the excitement is about."

"Fuck him all you want," Guilo said, "as long as I get my hands on him eventually."

"How is Sergei going to adjust to a new master?" John asked. "Think he'll be resentful or anything silly like that?"

"No problem, John. Sergei is a slave through and through. He accepts his fate exactly as slaves are supposed to. He'll be a little surprised, and probably a little regretful in that he enjoys his supervisory position here and his access to all that good looking stock at any time, but once he realizes he's going to a similar position at your estate with you as his new master and that he'll still have access to a bunch of new slaves whenever he wants, he'll settle in fast enough and be grateful. Besides, he's told me he enjoys you ramming your big tool down his throat or up his ass when you visit. I can see that in view of some of the guests I have that he's ordered to bed down with," Guilo smiled as he reminded John of all the fat, ugly visitors Sergei had entertained, many of them short-changed when it came to sexual equipment and some so old they could barely get it up anymore even after hours of Sergei's gallant efforts.

"Well, Sergei's always turned me on. I don't know what this Santos looks like, but Sergei needn't take a back seat to most hunks on the marketplace. I guess I just like the best Poland has to offer," John laughed.

"Santos is Italian - he looks it and he acts it. He's friskier than Sergei, borders on arrogance for a slave, and is kind of swarthy. He may not turn you on at all, but at least give him a try. Knowing him, he'll be close to raping you anyway, he's so damn eager all the time."

"Sounds too aggressive for me, Guilo. But whatever turns you on."

"You'll see, John. By the time that little boat gets from Delos over to their privately owned island, he'll have you stripped and up his ass at least once, the rascal," Guilo laughed. "That's the way we Italians are."

"Bull shit," John chuckled. "I bought a young Italian slave a couple of years ago that's so lethargic he can barely get it up half the time, and, if he wasn't so good looking, I would have sold him off months ago. Frankly, he's not worth a damn in bed - not compared with what slave's half his price can do once they understand what you expect from them. He's all looks and no action - hung like a horse, built like a bull, and looks like a Greek God. But what good is it if you're a dud in bed?"

"When are you going on this big buying trip?" Guilo asked. "I can hardly wait to bed Santos down here in his native country."

"I'll call and set it up as soon as you get off the damn phone line," John Morgan chuckled. "You forget I've dealt with Guiliano Imports many times over the years. I'm sure they'll bust a gut to accommodate me."

"You got me trading with them," Guilo confirmed.

"You and many others throughout the world," John Morgan said with some satisfaction. "They won't cheat one of their old customers."

The caged British slave listening to all of this swallowed hard around his penis gag and realized there was no way he would soon be back on the streets of his home town where he'd been abducted just eight days ago. Already, judging from the phone conversation, he'd been somewhere in Italy and back. Now, apparently, he was going to some island somewhere close to another place he'd never heard of, Delos, wherever that was, and was a place where slaves were trained for future owners, including, it seemed, open use of their bodies for their owner's sexual pleasures. Tears of despair ran down his cheeks for the third time since the phone conversation had started and, despite himself, he couldn't get rid of his enormous erection as the huge butt plug within him rubbed against his prostate every time he even breathed. It seemed like he was already losing control of his body.

———————

John Morgan landed on the airstrip in Delos in the small jet he owned for just such excursions. Carefully stowed in the luggage compartment was his overnight case and the cage holding his plugged property, the newly enslaved British construction worker. Whipping out his cell phone even before he unstrapped himself from the pilot's seat, he called 03-881-5644-012 as instructed.

"Guiliano Imports," a pleasant, deep voice answered. "How can I be of help?"

"John Morgan, Eduardo. I've just landed at Delos and need the boat. I've got my trade-in with me."

"A good flight, I assume, John?" Eduard Guiliano responded pleasantly. "I've alerted Aristo Mythos to make all the arrangements for your visit. You remember Aristo, don't you, John? I can't recall if he was here on your last visit or if he was off on a buying trip."

"No, Eduardo, he was there, but it's been a while. Who's picking me up?"

"A slave named Santos, the one you were specifically interested in buying, John. I thought you might as well look him over good on the boat coming over. But, as I told you, John, he's one of our main slave overseers, so his purchase price is quite high. Although," Eduardo chuckled, "I'm sure you could buy him if anyone could. He'll be at the airstrip in just a few minutes - I've already signaled him you've arrived. I'll see you as soon as you're over here on the island."

At that moment, a BMW station wagon arrived and parked next to the luggage compartment of the plane. As the driver emerged and smiled brightly, dressed in a light blue turtle-necked shirt, form fitting gray slacks, and white deck shoes, John Morgan could see why his friend Guilo was so enamored with this beautiful specimen of manhood. He was, all in one, stunningly handsome, ruggedly masculine, and projected a total willingness to please.

"Welcome back to Guiliano Imports, sir" the man said cheerfully, helping the visitor out of the plane's exit with a slight bow. "May I transfer your luggage and the delivered goods into the station wagon while you get comfortable. I've left the engine on so the air conditioning is running and there's a chilled bottle of wine waiting for you in the back seat."

"Santos?" Mr. Morgan asked.

"Yes...master," the man said with his eyes lowered to the ground. "How may I serve you?"

"Mr. Parsimi, the Italian count who visited here about six months ago, spoke most highly of you," John Morgan said as he reached forward and lifted the man's head to study his face. The slave automatically thrust his pelvis forward since he was being inspected. "Oh, and yes, transfer everything out of the luggage compartment into the car. Both items go to the island with us."

"Yes, master," Santos said as he waited until Mr. Morgan had finished inspecting his face and then bolted into action. Within minutes, he was in the driver's seat after lifting the heavy cage onto a wheeled cargo carrier and then again lifting it into the back of the station wagon along with the carrier. Despite his efforts, he was breathing only slightly hard, but had noted with interest the caged slave's nose ring had been fastened tightly to the bars of the cage. "Would you like a tour of the island or would you like to proceed directly to Guiliano's private island, master?"

"I've seen Delos before, so let's get over to Eduardo's private retreat where I can change my clothes and relax."

"Yes, master," Santos said as he sped away from the airstrip, keeping silent until prompted as he had been taught.

"How long have you been serving the Guilianos, Santos?" Mr. Morgan asked.

"For about eight years now, master."

"Don't you get bored on that little island?" Mr. Morgan asked.

"Sometimes, master, but I have many assignments that keep me busy and, of course, I meet many potential buyers who visit the island on a regular basis," the slave answered enthusiastically.

"Well, the Italian count who visited here some months ago spoke quite highly of you, Santos," John Morgan continued. "Seemed you help him select six slaves he wanted for litter bearers, all matched by physique and height. And, as I recall, he enjoyed using you as well - in fact, he still talks about it now and then," he chuckled.

"Thank you, master," Santos said graciously, "but most visitors are able to use my body, along with all of the Guiliano Import properties, for their enjoyment - it's one of the small perks you expect in visiting Guiliano Imports. All Guiliano slaves are taught to expect nothing less and enjoy pleasing our master's guests."

"And when can this guest start enjoying your body?"

"Would you like to use me now?" Santos said eagerly. There's a deserted clump of trees and a bed of soft grass right ahead that should be most comfortable for you to use my body."

"Well, since you put it that way, how can I refuse, but we'll wait until we're on the boat," Mr. Morgan said as he started to loosen his belt.

"That won't be more than a few more minutes," Santos turned and gave the new guest a huge smile. "I hope I'm as good for you as the Italian count remembered."

"He also said you were pretty arrogant for a slave," John Morgan warned as he studied the back of the handsome slave's head. "I'm afraid I'm not as tolerant a master as Count Parsimi."

"No master," Santos said humbly. "I'm sorry if I offended you."

"You can make it up to me when we're on the boat," Mr. Morgan responded with a chuckle.

"Yes, master," Santos said ardently.

As the car zoomed along, Mr. Morgan asked, "What did you think of the British slave I brought with me?"

"Very nice looking, master, and well hung. Once he's cleaned up and body shaved, he should be most presentable. Has he been trained, master?" Santos said brightly.

"With his nose ring pinioned to the cage bars and plugged at both ends? Hardly!" John Morgan chortled.

"Well, Master, he's going to the right place to be trained properly," Santos said with conviction. "He'll be no problem in a few months at the most."

"Well, I suppose you're right, but, right now, the slave is most uncooperative."

"As I'm sure you already know, Master, the Guiliano's training program will correct that problem within a week," Santos said with assurance.

"So fast?" Mr. Morgan asked. "Even for those new to slavery?"

"Yes, master. Once the new properties realize all their needs, including every morsel of food and every drink of water is under their new owners jurisdiction, they begin to realize the boundaries of their new existence. Add to that the constant threat of pain so severe they never even imagined it could hurt so much, and the overwhelming feeling of helplessness as they're branded, repeatedly raped, constantly naked, fitted with collars, rings, and restraining bands, and not even allowed to talk, and it doesn't take long to realize you're a slave now, not the human being you used to be. Once you realize all of that, the real training can commence."

"I can tell you're a slave trainer, Santos," John Morgan commented. "You seem to know all about what goes on in a slave's head. Is that because of your experience as a trainer or your experience as a slave?"

"Both, master. That's why the best trainers of slaves are slaves themselves if I may say so."

As promised, the speeding BMW was at the dock within a few minutes and Santos helped Mr. Morgan board the boat before lugging the heavy cage from the back of the station wagon onto the yacht's main deck with the caged slave positioned so that he was forced to see both Santos and his master. It was obvious the house slave was tremendously strong. It was also obvious he had transferred many a slave to the luxurious boat in that he quickly returned the cargo carrier to the back of the station wagon before locking the car up in a nearby parking space so it would be ready for his next trip over to Delos and its convenient airplane and yacht facilities. Quickly upon his return, he started the diesel engines, guided the yacht out of the small harbor and, adjusting a few controls, turned on the auto-pilot. Once that was done, he quickly turned to his new master.

"Master, may I speak?" he asked humbly.

"Make it short - you know I want to fuck you now," John Morgan said impatiently.

"Do you want me to cover the new slave's cage, master, or is it alright if he starts learning immediately what is expected of a Guiliano property. There is no better way to learn the proper role of a slave, master, than to watch a well-trained slave in action."

"And that well-trained slave would be you, I suppose?" John Morgan laughed heartedly at the effrontery of the Italian slave trainer. "Well, if you're so damn confident you'd be the perfect model to follow for the poor slave chained by his nose there, I suppose I'm confident enough to play the role of the demanding master, because, Santos, I expect your best efforts in servicing me."

"Yes, master," Santos replied with a winsome smile. "That's exactly what I plan to give you - my very best effort and... then some," he added seductively. With that, he stripped, carefully folding each piece of clothing and placing it in a built-in wardrobe in the pilot's compartment where it would be ready and waiting for his next exit at Delos.

John Morgan thoroughly enjoyed watching the magnificent Italian slave slip out of his clothes which the slave did with prescient seductive grace, well aware he was being studied by the English visitor. First he slipped out of the deck shoes and then removed the turtle-necked shirt revealing first his handsome tall tight-fitting brass collar neatly engraved with "Santos" all around the edge with "Property of Guiliano Imports" right beneath the name. Next you couldn't help but notice his magnificent musculature and smooth olive-colored skin, highlighted by bulging pecs, a smart looking "G" Guiliano brand on his right pec, well-shaped large brown nipples, each fitted with 2" brass rings that matched his collar and his beautiful washboarded stomach muscles. As he turned to hang the shirt up in the locker, his muscular back structure was fully displayed, tapering down to a small waist surprisingly small for such a muscular, well-built man. Turning to face the island's new guest, he slipped out of his gray slacks which fit him like a glove. Sans any underwear, quickly revealed was a beautifully shaped bubble butt, strong, muscular thighs and calves, and, center stage, a 12 x6" circumcised cock perfectly shaped atop two huge balls. The entire package, totally smooth from a recent body shave, protruded markedly due to the thick brass band welded around it, again engraved with "Property of Guiliano Imports." As Santos turned to carefully hang his pants up, another brand, identical to the one on his right chest, was displayed on his left rump. Despite himself, John Morgan took in his breath at the sight - the slave was, indeed, absolutely magnificent, the perfect embodiment of masculine appeal. He could understand Guilo's attraction toward the slave and his almost obsessive desire to own the animal.

Santos smiled beautifully and said, "Would the master like me on my knees for a good sucking first, or on my back for a good fucking? Or perhaps on my hands and knees if you prefer to fuck me Greek style?"

A strange strangled noise came from the caged slave a few feet away who had an astonished look on his face as he slowly began to understand the total degradation and absolute shame he would have to endure prior to abandoning all his previous beliefs, values, and assumptions as to what was right and wrong in this world. Only then, he thought, could he ever casually and openly display his body to an absolute stranger, let alone cheerily discuss how one's body was to be utilized for some unknown 'master's' pleasure. Neither Santos nor John Morgan paid the slightest attention to the new property in the cage, no matter what strange noises emerged despite its penis gag.

Reaching for his belt, John Morgan quickly slipped out of his own clothes, letting them fall to the floor in his haste. "Are you lubed, slave?"

"Yes, master. All Guiliano properties are kept lubricated at all times for our guest's convenience."

"Well, Santos, on your knees and get me completely lathered, then get on your hands and knees with your knees spread wide so your hole is completely accessible. I think I'll start out by delivering a good load up your ass."

"Yes, master," Santos said cheerfully as he sunk to his knees and quickly slurped down John Morgan's sizeable instrument in one gulp, going clear down to the root to make sure his saliva would cover the entire instrument before pumping up and down on the swollen prick until it reached a full, throbbing erection. As he did so, his eyes never left his master of the moment so that he could fully judge the reactions to his efforts.

"Um...um... very nice, slave," John Morgan said as he fully enjoyed the velvety mouth sucking away on him. "Take it all the way down your throat, slave, and work those throat muscles on it."

The slave, unable to talk, moaned in affirmative response and quickly slid the large prick well down his oral cavity until he felt his throat muscles spasm around the invading shaft.

"That's right, Santos," Mr. Morgan said as his prick felt as if it were being rhythmically milked by the slave's throat muscles. "Keep at it boy - swallow it all the way down. That's it, Santos," he ordered as he gripped the handsome slave's head in his hands. "Just keep at it, slave. I'm going to unload down your throat and then, on the next round, I'll fuck your ass."

"Umm..." was all Santos could say, but he suctioned until his cheeks were drawn inward as his throat muscles continued the massage of the master's tool.

The British slave could hardly escape the unbelievable display in front of him with his nose ring fastened tightly to the cage's bars. He had heard the term "cocksucker," of course, but he never dreamed it involved somehow overcoming your natural gag reflex, taking a man's prick clear down deep into your throat, working your throat muscles around the strange intrusion, and then obviously swallowing all of a man's seed. And to do so without force, even eagerly, seemed unreal in the naive world he had come from. He was sure even his fellow construction workers, hardly innocent in the ways of the world, would never believe the scene now playing out in front of him. He was so astonished he could do nothing but stare.

Within the minute, John Morgan arched his back, jammed the slave's head down as far as it would go on his prick, gasped loudly, and shot the first of a volley of five loads down the slave's throat and into his stomach. The slave in turn sucked for all he was worth, breathing rapidly as best he could through his nose, his mouth stretched to the breaking point. By the next minute, Mr. Morgan was wet with sweat, panting, and slowly sliding his now semi-erect prick out of the slave's mouth as he released the slave's head from his grip simultaneously.

As soon as he could again speak, Santos quickly said, "Thank you, master... Thank you," before cleaning his master's tool completely with his active tongue, swallowing all the residue down his throat and into his stomach where it would join all the other cum of his master. Licking his lips off with his tongue, he asked, "Shall I position for your fucking me now, master, or would you prefer to rest a while first while, perhaps, playing with my tits or perhaps playing with my shaft and balls?"

"Eager little whore, aren't you?" John Morgan laughed. "But I would like to examine you. Stand up and put your hands in back of your neck with your pelvis thrust out - you know, the standard slave display position. I think I would like to play with your body a bit before continuing."

"Yes, master," Santos said lustily, quickly assuming the commanded position and positioning himself so that his own massive organs, now fully erect, were conveniently pressed into his new master's hands.

As John Morgan caressed the slave's big swollen balls and then began stroking the Italian's quivering erection, the slave moaned softly, as if in gratitude, but nevertheless noticed the British slave in the cage.

"Your slave's going to be easy to train," Santos commented as he thrust his genitals even more firmly into his master's massaging hands as a sign of his total compliance.

John Morgan temporarily glanced over at the slave, his nose ring still forcing his face to the cage bars facing them. The slave's eyes reflected total shock, but then he looked down and saw the slave had a huge erection.

"Your slave is excited just watching you get sucked off. I imagine he'll shoot when he sees you fuck me," he commented professionally. "If he does, he's what we call a 'natural'."

John Morgan churned Santos' balls more vigorously with his left hand as his right hand tightened its grip on the swollen shaft. Soon Santos broke out into a full sweat and was beginning to pant as he felt the familiar symptoms of an impeding orgasm.

"Do you want me to shoot now, master, or would you prefer to fuck me first?" Santos asked subserviently.

"Hold it, slave, until I give you permission to shoot," John Morgan said sternly. "I thought you were properly trained," he added for emphasis.

"Yes, master," was all Santos risked as an answer as his body coated itself with a fine sheen of sweat and his pelvis began slight humping motions he fought to control. He felt his balls pull themselves up close to his body despite the rough massage they were receiving from Mr. Morgan who kept pulling them down lower in their sac. He knew as long as his user forced his balls downward forcefully, he wouldn't shoot off. His training over the years had taught him that, but it also indicated this temporary master was sophisticated in the sexual use of his slaves. Nevertheless, just about when he thought he would orgasm despite everything, his user released his stimulating hands and ordered the slave to get onto his hands and knees for a good fucking. Santos immediately did so, making sure his legs were spread wide to best expose his hole and that he was positioned precisely for Mr. Morgan's convenience and ease in fucking him.

Both Santos and Mr. Morgan looked over at the caged slave as they positioned themselves. As Santos had predicted, the slave's prick was still fully erect and was now dripping pre-cum, but the look of resigned incredulity was still on the boy's face.

With no preliminaries, John Morgan drove his long, thick shaft well up into the Italian slave's open chute and then, with a few deep thrusts, thrust the last few inches all the way into the slave. Santos groaned sensuously in acknowledgment of a master's total possession of his body and wiggled his butt a little to better accommodate the huge tool stretching his anal chute. He was well familiar with having his hole opened for the pleasure of others, but he seldom had one fill him so completely outside of the huge training dildos he'd learned on years ago. As the new master began pumping him vigorously, he tightened his ass muscles around the invading tool and began a pumping motion of his own, perfectly coordinating his pelvic movements with those of his user so that maximum penetration and pleasure of his master could be achieved. The feeling brought back memories of his original slave training and he smiled at the recollection of how he used to scream, and then buck and snort as the huge training dildos were rammed up him one by one, imagining he was being torn apart by the assault. As Mr. Morgan picked up his pace, driving deeply into him with each thrust, Santos reflected on how much wiser he was now that he had a little experience. He knew he could stretch to accommodate about anything up his ass anymore without bodily damage (although he was often mighty sore afterwards); the pain he used to scream about was no longer there once he had been properly opened but had, in fact, been replaced with a sensual feeling of fullness which was usually quite arousing; and, if he clenched his ass muscles to best service his user, he often, if his master allowed it, orgasmed himself, often about the same time as the master shot their own load well up inside him.

At that moment of reflection, Mr. Morgan arched his back, and moaned loudly as he drove completely into the slave underneath him and discharged fully in a series of spasms until white cum was flowing out from the embedded prick and down the thighs of the slave being fucked. Santos, well familiar with the feeling of being packed with hot thick cum to the point of overflow, was soaked with sweat once again and felt his own prick twitching in need, his own clear pre-cum pooling underneath him.

"Master, may I cum?" Santos gasped in desperate need.

"Go for it boy, you've earned it," John Morgan said magnanimously

Instantly, Santos shot load after load of steaming thick cum down on the deck floor beneath him, groaning in relief. It took six separate discharges before his balls were emptied, leaving a huge mess on the deck coating both his hands and knees.

As Mr. Morgan withdrew his large tool from Santos' butt, he laughed as he saw Santos' output and his own cum running down the slave's thighs. "Lick that mess up, boy, and wipe your legs off before we slip and break our leg after you've cleaned me, of course," he laughed.

"Thank you, master, thank you," Santos said as he instantly put his mouth to his master's tool and quickly cleaned all the residue off with a vigorous tongue washing, swallowing the flecks of cum, lubricant, and ass juices without hesitation. That completely done, he put his mouth to the deck and used his tongue to slurp up his own steaming cum. Within a minute, he had managed to lick the deck dry and was busily swallowing his own load. With his finger, he scooped his users cum off of his legs and nosily slurped that down also, announcing with each finger full that his master's donation was "delicious."

"What are you thanking me for, Santos? The nice snack of hot cum or being generously allowed to unload?" Mr. Morgan asked.

"Both, master. I haven't been allowed to unload for almost three days now, and for me that's a long time with all the usage I get. But, in addition, I haven't been fed today - there simply wasn't time with all the new slaves and your arrival and such, so all that cum was especially good on an empty stomach, master. If I may say so, master, your cum is particularly tasty."

"You are a whore through and through, Santos," Mr. Morgan chuckled. "A connoisseur of cum as well, I see."

"Yes, master. There are differences in cum, master, as I'm sure you're well aware owning many slaves over the years which I'm sure you've milked from time to time. But your cum, master, is fresh and almost sweet tasting."

"Well, I'm glad you like it. Behave yourself, and I'll let you have another snack or so before I leave."

"Thank you, master," Santos said with sincere gratitude, licking his lips in anticipation of the bonus meals.

Just then, the caged British slave moaned around his penis gag and arched his back as best he could within the constraint forced upon him by his leashed nose ring. Santos and his master both looked over to see the Brit, bright red in shame and embarrassment and with his hairy body covered in sex sweat, spewing load after load of steamy white cum all over his belly, chest, neck and face which slowly, due to its thickness, began dripping onto the cage floor.

"You were right, Santos," Mr. Morgan chuckled. "The boy is a natural slave - and a bit of a whore to boot, I'd say."

"He'll be an easy one to train for sexual use," Santos observed, "but he'll need to be broken before he'll obey instantly, without question, any command given him - at least outside a master's bedroom. In a master's bed, he's a natural and will settle in easily to his new life."

"You mean he's homosexual by nature, Santos?" Mr. Morgan asked in curiosity as to how Santos would know such a thing.

"Not necessarily, master, not that it matters now that he's a slave. He'll do what he is told to do regardless, master, of course.

But I meant he's a sexual animal and it doesn't matter what he thinks of himself - he'll do whatever is necessary to get off whenever he can - with a man, with a women, with a horse... It doesn't matter, master. His sex drive is just too strong for him to hold back any longer. In a master or mistress' bed, he's just a tamed animal from now on. Personally, I think he's heterosexual - most of them are, you know. But, as I said, it doesn't make a grain of difference once they're properly trained."

"What are you, Santos?"

"A slave, master, here for his master's bidding," Santos answered, rather confused.

"No, no... slave. Of course you're a slave, Santos. I meant your sexual preference before you were a slave."

"Oh, that, master. As I said, master, it makes no difference what you are once you're a slave, but, personally, I was originally heterosexual. But anymore, master, I'm not sure I really wasn't bisexual. I like servicing either sex too well to deny I enjoy both. Of course, before I was a slave, I didn't have the opportunities to explore my sexuality as I did in my slave training, master."

"Do you think that's true of most slaves, Santos, since you train them, I understand."

"Yes, master, I'm convinced all slaves are bisexual deep down inside. They just need to be opened up to it through a good training program."

"What about masters, Santos? Are they bisexual deep down inside, as you put it, too?"

"Masters can be anything they want, master. But with slaves so widely available for their use anymore, I imagine masters can explore all aspects of sexuality that those too poor to afford slaves can't do. If I may speak frankly, master, I think poor free folks are the only ones who fret about such matters anymore."

"Ah... a real thinker," John Morgan said admiringly as he reached over and began playing with Santos ringed tits until they were fully erect and swollen. "I like that in a slave."

"Yes, master," Santos replied as he thrust his chest out for more convenient handling by his master.

Once the tits were swollen to their full size, John Morgan sucked on first one and then the other a while before moving over to the caged British slave.

"Let's have a little snack to tide us over before we're at your home, Santos," John Morgan said in invitation as he reached into the cage and wiped a large portion of the slave's fresh cum onto his finger and then, inserting in his mouth, rolled the cum around a while to thoroughly evaluate it for taste and consistency. "Um... strong... tangy... and very thick. Go ahead, help yourself... You said you were hungry."

"Yes, master," Santos said as he scooped another string of cum off of the slave's belly and quickly placed it in his mouth.

"Well, slave?" Mr. Morgan said as he watched Santos churn the cum around in his mouth.

"Too strong and acidic for most buyers, master, but the slave's taste will change once he's been on a steady diet of slave chow for a while. He'll taste more like me once his diet is totally controlled. The new slave chows are formulated to produce a nice taste to a slave's cum as well as give a pleasant non-offensive herbal odor to the slave's sweat. Guiliano Imports only uses the new slave chows for that very reason, master."

"I'll get the brand names down before I leave, Santos," Mr. Morgan commented. "I do like the taste of your sauce and your body smell is really quite pleasant, even when you're in full sweat."

"Thank you, master," Santos replied. "The feed we use is Purina's standard slave chow but get the bags marked 'new and improved,' master."

"Thanks for the tip. I use Purina usually anyway - its as cheap as anything and it keeps the slaves healthy enough. But I'm not sure I'm into the new and improved yet. Next batch, I'll make sure."

As the Italian slave and his master finished enjoying the last remnants of the British slave's cum off of his body and off the bottom of the cage, the yacht autopilot signaled that it was going into docking procedures and would require manual assist. Santos took one last dollop of slave cum off of the cage floor and savored it as he returned to the pilot's controls. Within one minute, the yacht was dockside, and huge, muscular naked black slaves, appearing out of nowhere, leaped aboard to secure the boat and unload both the caged slave as well as Mr. Morgan's overnight case. Each bore the "G" brand on their chests and rumps, each was magnificently built, each was unusually handsome in different ways, and each was hung like a horse. When Mr. Morgan walked across the gangplank onto Guiliano's island, all the slaves, including Santos, knelt near the gangplank, their legs spread wide to best expose their sizable genitals, their chests thrust out for full display, their muscles tensed, and with their hands clasped around their neck collars to best display their musculature. Each of their heads were bowed as far as their tall slave collars would allow.

"Welcome to Guiliano Imports," a swarthy well dressed man said extending his hand. "We've met before, John. I'm Aristo Mythos, the manager here.

"Yes, Aristo, I recall the last time we met wasn't here on the island, but in London, as I recall. You said you were looking over a large lot of Gaelic slaves being offered by some dealer there. Did you have any luck?"

"What a good memory you have, John," Aristo Mythos said admiringly. "Yes, I did luck out on that trip. Bought the whole lot of them. In fact, you're welcome to look them over here. They're just finishing up their training regimen and getting polished for an upcoming auction."

"Well, I just might do that if I have time, Aristo," John replied.

"I know you're here to buy six slaves of a particular shade and all the exact same physique, John." Aristo was noted for getting right to the point. "You wanted a creamy milk-chocolate brown, very muscular physiques, and all the same height and weight. I assume you want them to be good looking and attractive in both face and body, black haired to match their racial characteristics, smooth skinned and practically naturally hairless as most of that color are anyway, but, John, you didn't mention their sexual organs. Do you want them all the same size both flaccid and erect? If they're going to be used to power this new slavemobile contraption of yours, it would probably be a good idea if they're displayed while they're working away in the contraption. Besides, John, I'm sure you intend to use them around your house and in your bed when they're not engaged in this fancy contraption of yours."

"Slow down, Aristo," John laughed. "You're going too fast for me to keep up. Let's see, you have it all right down to your first question. Yes, I want them all very heavy hung and all about alike if I can get them that way. It would be nice if they could be within an inch of each other on their dicks if they're all nice and thick anyway.

And, yes, they'll only be working the machine at most a few hours each day. The rest of the time I intend to have them fully displayed as they clean the house, do all the lawn and gardening around the estate, wait tables, and use their bodies to entertain my guests and myself, of course. They'll be worked hard, Aristo, in that I only have four other slaves on hand now after the trade-in I brought with me."

"You're going to need a slave handler with 10 slaves on hand, John. Are you going to buy a trained handler here or did you have other plans?" Aristo said professionally.

"No, Aristo, I'm going to buy a handler from you," John said with a smirk, "as you well know," looking pointedly as the bowed head of Santos beside them.

"I just wanted that confirmed," Aristo laughed. "The property will be horribly expensive. I assume you were impressed with the proposed property on the trip over."

"Yes, most memorable, but I must confess I will have little more than the paperwork on the property after a few days. Count Parsimi is giving me a long-term loan of his most able manager, the Polish slave Sergei, in exchange for the loan of my new property which he is most desirous of having for a while. The new property will be mine legally, but any use I get will be in the next day or so... not counting, of course... so far."

"Well, in the interim, I shall make sure you have complete access to the new property if you don't find something else around here even more to your liking. Recalling your tastes, I think some of the new slaves I have lined up for your inspection will be equally, if not even more, attractive to you than the new handler we're discussing. You've always had a preference for fine looking black stock, John, and I've got some I hope you're really going to appreciate."

"Always the salesman, aren't you Aristo," John laughed. "And what's so great about these blacks you're talking about? The slaves displaying themselves at our feet right now are quite a turn-on. But they're too black to be in the lot I said I wanted, Aristo."

"Yes, yes, John. I'm well aware of that. I just thought you might like to bed one of these boys down before you left - no charge of course. All of our stock here on the island is available at any time for your use. These black slaves here are great in bed. I've used them myself many a time and they're consistently good in their duties."

John looked down at the beautiful absolutely hairless black slaves once again, their heads bowed in submission as much as their thick collars would allow, their chest thrust out to best display their sculptured pecs and meaty ringed tits, their large banded semi-erect sexual organs fully displayed between their wide spread legs. He motioned for them to stand up in standard display position and then proceeded to knead their balls and massage their shafts into full erection one by one. That done, he pinched their tits between his thumb and forefinger to test for reaction, and was pleased to see each and every black slave's tits swell instantly into a full erection due to the fondling. He then stuck his finger in each of their mouths and admired the strong sucking action each elicited in response, admiring their handsome smooth skinned faces as he did so, each set of eyes pleading for him to use them.

"Aristo, you've made an offer I can't refuse. How about having two of them to service me as soon as I've taken a shower and the other two sent to my room around bedtime. That is, unless I find something more interesting by then."

"You probably will, John, but it won't matter. If not tonight for the other two, I'll have them cleaned up and ready for you first thing in the morning for a little morning exercise."

The four black slaves being discussed so openly seemed relieved the new guest wanted to use them and smiled broadly as their forthcoming usage in his bed was being planned.

"Santos, take Mr. Morgan to Guest Suite #1 along with his luggage. The blacks can handle the new slave he's trading in."

"Yes, Master Mytho," Santos said as he quickly rose, still stark naked, picked up the leather overnight case, and, pointing toward the guests suites, heeled behind the island's latest guest.

"I can see from some dried cum on Santos' leg he obviously wasn't aware was still there that you have sampled what the Italian has to offer our guests," Aristo called after them. "He's even better once you get him in a real bed. Enjoy the slave again before you shower without the time pressures of a yacht trip. I'll see you in my office when you're all freshened up - say a couple of hours - and I'll show you what I had in mine for your next purchases."

"I see your hospitality hasn't slipped a bit," John Morgan said as he quickly left for the assigned suite, Santos just a step or so behind, his muscular, branded bubble-butt churning alluringly as he followed.

Two hours later, John Morgan was freshly showered, shaved, and in a new set of clothes laid out for him by Santos when the slave had unpacked his luggage prior to servicing his new master. After a one-and-a-half hour romp with this epitome of masculine sexual appeal, as well as the two black slaves sent to his suite only minutes after he had settled in, John Morgan felt totally drained, completely satisfied, and at peace with the world. He doubted if he could ever get a full erection again, but knew better. Santos took the heavy usage in stride and was hopeful he had met his new master's expectations. Not being allowed this time around to alleviate his own needs, his prick was hard and quivering, pre-cum leaking out just a little. As soon as his master had left, he sent the two well-used blacks back to the slave quarters, then showered again as ordered, and put some soothing antiseptic lotion on his swollen tits, (a fixture in every guest suite along with brass cleaner and clear lubricating jelly) since masters often bit or squeezed a little too hard in their enthusiasm. He polished his collar, rings, and genital band to its original gleam, lubed himself thoroughly once again, and then quickly reported to the slave sales room where he knew he would be needed shortly.

"John, it's taken some real searching among the stock, but I think I've got exactly what you're looking for," Aristo said enthusiastically. "It just so happened a large batch of North African stock was just finishing their training regimen when your request came in. I used our databases to match up their numbers with height and weight requirements, penis size, skin shade, etc., and got it down to about 35 or so. Then I went down to the holding pens and picked them out by hand. You know, skin shade varies a lot according to the light they're displayed in, and some slaves vary from one part of their body to another. And a computer can't really tell you much about overall appeal or what the musculature looks like - it just records the body mass index which tells you a lot, but doesn't really tell you what the finished product looks like. Well, anyway, I've got eight slaves down in the holding pens that look almost like twins, I tell you, and all are damn sexy, at least to me, and all are a creamy chocolate brown with skin as smooth as a baby's bottom. I think you're going to like them. If not... well. John, we've got thousands on hand this time of year, all fully trained so I'm sure you'll find something. Shall be have a look-see? I've had them moved over to the sales room which is a lot more pleasant than the holding pens and where Santos, if he can still walk, can display them properly."

"Well organized, as always, Aristo," John laughed. "Let's go to the sales room, as you suggest, but I'm not sure about Santos. When I left, he was just crawling into the showers as I'd ordered him to, sporting a huge hard on. I didn't let him shoot off because I didn't know what your plans were for him later in the day."

"Very thoughtful, John," Aristo said as he walked toward the door with John following him. "Especially since Santos is one of the slaves up for sale this afternoon, although he doesn't realize it yet. It will give you a chance to look him over thoroughly before making a final decision about him. Let me assure you he's about as good a slave trainer and handler as you can find. He's had more experience than his age would indicate, and, as I hope you know by now, he's unparalleled in servicing either a master or mistress. He's never caused us one bit of trouble and, as he'll readily admit, he loves being a slave. You set that boy free and he'll be right back in his collar before you could say scat. Most people think he's about as good looking as a man gets and he takes pride in being a 'natural whore' as he calls it. But, because of all that, the slave is about as expensive as slaves get these days. So, before you plunk down all that money, look him over very well to make sure you want that kind of investment. If you buy Santos, John, that's one hell of a loan you're making to Count Parsimi. This Sergei he's loaning you in return, who isn't Guiliano stock, must really be something."

"He is, Aristo, whether you trained him or not. Guilo's owned him for years and is quite fond of the slave. He's powerfully built, very nice looking, and totally subservient to a master. He too seems to enjoy being a slave and I'm sure he would never want to not be owned by someone or other after all those years as a slave. The way I understand it, Sergei was sold when he was just short of 19 years old by a German slave dealer to the Count. Although he was fairly well trained by the German merchant, Guilo spent considerable time honing him to perfection as a slave, using, he tells me, a strong whip, food deprivation, and frequent fuckings to mold him to his needs. By the time he was 20 he was well nigh perfect according to Guilo, but really reached his zenith when Guilo put him in charge of his other slaves. He's managed that team of litter bearers you sold to

Guilo beautifully - the slaves practically worship him and he has them shaped up to Guilo's needs wonderfully. They're milked daily, fucked frequently, and suck off Guilo's guests regularly without a whiff of concern. And, of course, they have to do back breaking work hauling that heavy litter around every day chained by their tits and ordered to show hard all the time they're fashioned to the litter. Despite all that, the slaves you sold Guilo are happy as a lark and will do anything to please either Sergei or their master."

"What this Sergei like in bed?" Aristo asked professionally.

"In the same league as Santos, only not quite as openly whorish," John replied. "After we trade, I doubt if Sergei will disappoint me but I'm also fairly sure Santos will please the Count so well that Guilo will never ask for Sergei back."

"You say Count Parsimi's slaves are chained by their tits to the litter?" Aristo laughed. "And they have to show hard all the time they're carrying the damn thing?"

"Yep," John replied. "Their tits get all red and swollen, of course, after a while on the litter with the restraining chains pulling on their tit rings all the time but they seem to be used to it by now - at least they're able to show hard all the time, no matter what. Guilo told me it took about six weeks before they could show hard more than a hour or so, what with all the strain on their bodies, but they've got it down pat now. I never once saw them loose an erection at a weekend retreat I was at a week or so ago."

"I'll share that information with our trainers. They need to know just what owners expect out of Guiliano slaves nowadays."

"Yes, but seeing is believing," John said. "You should visit yourself. I'm sure Guilo would be honored if you visited him at his estate not too far from Rome. He thinks most highly of your products now that he owns some."

"I'd like to. Would I impose too much if I asked you to finagle an invitation from the Count?"

"Not if you make Santos affordable," John shot back.

"It's a deal," Aristo smiled as he opened the door to the sales room.

The room was exactly as John remembered it: row after row of cages stacked one on top of another, almost all holding a naked specimen within its cramped confines. If he remembered correctly, the cages were arranged by size, color, general appeal, and price with the most expensive goods close to the entrance. Although the room was spotlessly clean and beautifully furnished for visitor's comfort, it still had a slight smell of human sweat, semen, and, unavoidably, a whiff of urine, all mixed together. Nevertheless, it was considerably less smelly than most slave markets John was familiar with in England and the rest of Europe, especially rooms holding thousands of slaves all primed for inspection.

Santos, again semi-erect in all his glory, appeared instantly and sunk to his knees with his eyes lowered to the ground. "Masters," he greeted them.

"Do you want to look around, John, or just get right with inspection of the ones I picked out?" Aristo said as he casually ran his hand through Santos hair. "It's fine if you want to look around a bit first - I always enjoy looking at the current crop up for sale. Sometimes I find something interesting for bed that night."

"If I were in your shoes with all this stock available, I'd probably just fuck them on the spot rather than wait until evening," John laughed. "You're sated, Aristo, you know that, I suppose."

"Possibly, John. It's a small perk of my job."

"Well, not to keep you waiting, let's look at your selections, Aristo," John said. "I've got to start somewhere."

"Santos," Aristo said sharply.

The Italian slave leaped to his feet and disappeared behind a row of cages, followed by the squeak of cage doors, bare feet hitting the ground, and a few grunts and groans as the slaves stretched to alleviate their cramped muscles from the close confinement in the tiny cages where they were forced to sit with their head bent over between their crunched up legs and their arms fitting wherever there was room. Within a minute or so, to allow the slaves to stretch enough so they could walk on their own, Santos, with a slave whip now in his hand, herded the eight selected slaves onto the large display platform and ordered them, with a sharp crack of his whip barely over their heads, for all of them to assume the standard display position (legs wide apart; muscles tensed, hands in back of their head, pelvis and chest thrust forward).

Aristo had been right. They looked almost like clones of one another. Each was exactly the same shade of a creamy, almost glowing, chocolate brown; all had beautifully shaped piercing dark eyes with very long thick lashes unusual in men; all were markedly handsome in a very masculine way with square jaw lines, high cheekbones, and thin lips; all had skin as smooth and flawless as a baby; all were exactly the same height and sported the same heavy layering of muscle on muscle; each had prominent tits on massively muscular chests, and each had a nicely rounded, protruding butt. Further down, each sported a heavily knotted muscled abdomen, big almost black balls close to the body, and long, thick circumcised pricks exactly the same shape and all a darker brown than their skin hide. Each was quickly reaching full erection now that they were being displayed - a sure sign they were properly trained for the sales room. When fully erect, they would be classified as high grade studs by any auction house in the world.

John was startled at both their beauty and their sameness. He studied each body carefully to make sure his eyes weren't deceiving him as Santos ordered the slaves to slowly rotate one by one for his full inspection, including showing the potential buyer their hole, and lifting their balls to illustrate how large they were. Once his shock was over, he routinely ran his hand lightly over their muscles, pinched their tits to test for reaction, churned the large balls and then weighed them in the palm of his hand, stroked the slave to see how long it took for the first drop of pre-cum to appear and, again, fondled their tits to test for any hint of resistance to being handled in this fashion. Finally, he turned them around, felt the layers of muscle on their backs, squeezed their butts to test for firmness while running his finger over their Guiliano brand, and, ordering them to bend over, inserted a 12x6 dildo up their hole which Santos had ready, already properly greased to prevent any damage to the slave being inspected. Each slave accepted the full length and girth of the huge dildo with practiced skill, only grunting and moaning as the monster was rammed up them, but without a sign of resistance or resentment. Indeed, all of the slaves eventually pushed back on the dildo being rammed up them as a symbol of their acceptance of such usage and managed to smile when it was completely in place as a signal any pain caused by the intrusion was manageable. It was obvious the slaves were very well trained and eager to find a new owner.

"Are they voice-trained?" John asked as he pumped a dildo in and out of the last slave being examined.

"Better," Aristo said.

"Better? How?" John asked.

"They've been silenced. Best things for blacks like this who can turn into chatterboxes if you're not careful. We warned them in their first days here, but they continued to yell and scream in their early training and were always trying to whisper to each other in their pens at night despite being told not to do so. The trainers got tired of it and asked me if they could silence them. We snipped their vocal chords and now all they can do is grunt, but they can still indicate if they understand your command or if something is seriously wrong with their body or if they need medical attention, so no harm done. On the contrary, you'll find it adds considerably to their resale value if you tire of them. We're silencing more and more slaves these days due to market demands."

"What's their provenance, Aristo?" John asked.

"That's the best part of it, John," Aristo answered with considerable ebullience. "The reason they look so much alike is that all eight are half-brothers and are all 20 years old, being born within three months of each other."

John raised his eyebrows in confusion. "How could that be?"

"Well, it's sort of complicated, but, in essence, they all have the same daddy and their mommies were all sisters from one rather isolated black family of slaves so their genes weren't all mixed up. Seems this nomadic Berber tribe in the Sahara made their living selling slaves basically just as they'd done for thousands of years. One batch of slaves, considerably darker than these boys here, contained a huge Mandingo family with eight daughters all of child bearing age. They also had a young French slave in their possession they had bought in some small town on the North African coast who was real good looking, built like a bull, and hung like a horse. They put their French slave to stud with the eight daughters and, within three months, all eight slave women were knocked up. When the brood was born, they were simply raised by the slave women until, inevitably, their mothers were sold off one by one but by then they were being trained by their masters for the demands of the market so they barely noticed their departure. Their daddy had been sold off to an American millionairess shortly after they were born who, they told me, later sold him to a businessman in Hong Kong who prided himself on his male harem of varying nationalities and races. By the time these eight slaves were full grown, their training was complete and they were marketed in a small Tripoli market by the tribe that raised them. An Italian dealer operating in Libya spotted them there, bought them up solely for resale and notified one of our agents of their availability. When the agent flew to Libya to look them over, he bought them on the spot and had them crated up and shipped here for more advanced training. So, John, you see they are half-brothers twice over - their mothers were all sisters and their daddy was the same stud. They're half Mandingo and half-French - hence the nice coloring and the almost Gallic features on their brown skin. Their Mandingo blood gives them their magnificent builds and those huge sexual organs; the Gallic blood gives them those thin lips and that almost feminine delicate look despite all those rippling muscles and huge pricks that are always ready to go."

"I'll take all eight if the price is right," John announced. "I know I said I just needed six and that's right, but I've decided to add a couple of spares since they are, as you say, perfectly matched. Besides, they're exactly what turns me on. Aristo, you know me like a book!"

"If you take all eight, I'll knock 10% off the price of each of them. That way, you're actually getting the last two for next to nothing. How's that?"

"Well, how much for the lot, Aristo?"

Aristo looked at Santos who immediately produced a calculator for his master.

"Rounded off, and with the 10% discount figured in, 1.9 million euros for all eight not counting delivery charges."

"I'll take them with me on the jet if we can cram all of them in," John said, "so we can forget about delivery charges. Is that the best you can give a long time customer who's referred several good customers to you?"

"Oh, all right," Santos laughed. "1.85 million euro for old times sake. Why is it I feel I'm practically giving you the blacks?"

"1.848 million and I throw in the raw British slave whose practically worthless until he's properly trained. That's letting you have him for a mere 20,000 euros. Once he's trained and you have his body in good shape for display, you should easily get at least 250,000 out of him. Actually, he's very good looking and has a great body that should sell well. That's a decent profit despite the fact he's going to take a lot of time in training. Aristo, I paid 30,000 for him straight off the streets. I'm not willing to lose more than 10,000 for a week's worth of trouble with him."

"1.848 million euro for all eight blacks and I get the ownership papers on the young Brit," Aristo announced. "Going once, going twice - sold," he laughed. "Now, about that other matter. Santos," he barked, "up on the sales podium with the blacks for a good inspection. Mr. Morgan has an interest in buying you."

"Yes, master," Santos gulped in surprise as he quickly complied, assuming the full display position as ordered. He managed to muster a bright smile for his potential new owner.

"No need to inspect Santos," John laughed. "After all, I fucked him silly less than an hour ago. How much?"

"Are you ready? I warned you he'd be expensive."

"How much, Aristo?"

"One million euro and not a cent less."

"Aristo," John howled, "that's more than half as much as all eight blacks cost together."

"Yes, and worth it on the open market. The slave is spectacular - you've admitted that yourself - he's perfectly trained - he loves his slavery - he's a natural whore - and, best of all, he's one of the best slave trainers we've ever had. It will be hard to replace him."

"A million it is, Aristo. I can't argue with all that," John Morgan responded. "What's the slave's probable resale value if it doesn't work out like I plan?"

"Probably a million in European or American markets," Aristo said, "so I don't think you would lose on the investment within the next few years or so. After that, he'll start to age and he'll start to depreciate, but don't we all," Aristo laughed.

"A total of 2.848 million euro, then, for all nine slaves?" John Morgan asked.

When Aristo nodded his acceptance, John said, "I'll have the money forwarded from my account this afternoon while it's still fresh on my mind. That way, you can get the ownership papers all completed before dinner."

"That's why I like you, John. You don't horse around. You make up your mind fast and then act upon your decision instantly. I just wish all customers were more like you."

"Maybe I should have asked you for more of a discount," John laughed. "As soon as I arrange the money transfer to your account,

I'd like to use my new Italian property before the afternoons up. All this handling slaves has got me ready to go again and I do want to get my fill of him before I hand him over to Guilo in a few days. Oh, and don't forget those two other black boys you promised would be delivered to my room this evening."

"You're indefatigable, John," Aristo chuckled. "Are you sure a mere 10 to 12 slaves in their sexual peak and trained specifically to satisfy a master's lust can keep you satisfied? But, the two blacks are already scheduled for your use this evening, along with Santos, of course, especially now that he's yours anyway."

"Master? May I speak?" Santos asked his new master.

"Keep it brief. I want to screw you in bed, not chat all day," John shot back.

"Is this Guilo you're handing me over to Count Guilo Parsimo?"

"If you must know, yes, Santos. I'm giving you to the Count on a long-term loan since he seemed obsessed with your charms."

Tears of sheer joy spilled down Santos cheeks. "Oh, thank you, Master. Thank you. He said someday he would buy me and, although I truly love it here with Master Mythos, it's always been a dream of mine." Realizing the impropriety of what he had just said, he quickly added, "If slaves dare to ever dream."

"Well, you and I both know they shouldn't. Besides, you're just on loan - I'm retaining full ownership."

"Yes, master," Santos said. "Thank you, master."

"Let me interrupt Santos' totally inappropriate comments on his recent sale," Aristo Mythos said icily matched by a steely look of reprimand which caused the Italian slave to blush in embarrassment and shame. "If you ask me a good solid beating would teach the slave some manners, but, of course, you're his owner now, John. But if he were still mine, he'd be taught to keep that mouth of his shut unless asked a direct question. It's always been a problem with him, John, and a sound beating at least once a week is the only way I've found to keep his manners in place. You can see the reason why we're silencing more and more of our stock, but it's not practical with slave trainers, of course. Oh... because of Santos' mouth, I almost forgot what I was going to say. Oh, yes. John, I need to get these new purchases of yours down to the slavefitter if you're going to be leaving us soon. The fittings are part of the purchase price, of course, here at Guiliano Imports and you can have any fittings you want. It's easiest to get it done here in that we have all the equipment and a fitter who knows exactly what he's doing so the property isn't damaged in any way."

"Thanks for reminding me, Aristo. We'll have all eight black slaves done the same: copper collars with leash rings front and back and both sides that will look good on that brown skin engraved just 'Slavemobile' on the first line and 'Property of John Morgan, Esq.' on the second line. Both tits ringed with matching copper 1" rings and a 1" copper ring in the septum of their nose that sticks out far enough to leash in that I know that's one way they're going to be fastened to this slavemobile contraption. And I want their package tightly banded with a 1" copper band with a leash ring on top engraved with just 'Property of John Morgan, Esq.' - no individual names in that they're just going to be part of a working team. Make sure you don't forget the leash rings - I know that's necessary for their installation in the slavemobile but I can't remember the particulars - just that they're going to be fastened in by their collar, their tit and nose rings, and their balls. I want them shaved bald along with a complete body shave, but leave their eyebrows and eventually I plan a neat little mustache behind their nose ring."

Aristo was busily putting all of this information into his Palm Pilot so it could instantly be forwarded to the slavefitter along with the slave's identification numbers. "And your new Italian slave?"

"Just like he is, but you'll need to change the ownership labels on his collar and genital band to his name just like you have it now but with 'On Loan to Count Guilo Parsimo by Morgan Enterprises, Ltd.' Will all of that fit on his genital band, Aristo?"

"No problem - there's a lot of girth on that slave's band," Aristo snickered.

"I'll have to put a new collar and band on him when I get him over to my own home ground at a later date," John said almost to himself.

"If you ever get him back from the Count," Aristo snickered again. "If this Polish slave Sergei pleases you as much as you think he will, my bet is that Santos here is going back to his native country permanently."

That said, Aristo checked his Palm Pilot inputs and then pressed a button to forward the information to the slavefitter.

"Santos," he ordered sharply. "Get your ass and these eight blacks down to the slavefitter. When he's done with you, tell the handlers to start preparing the blacks for shipment to England in the smallest cages he can get them into - your new master's jet isn't all that big - and make sure they're completely cleaned out and plugged for the trip. When you're sure they've understood exactly what they're to do with the blacks, you get your own pretty little ass with your brand new collar and band over to your new master's bed. He's eager to get into you again - it's always better when you own what you're fucking, don't you think, John? Just gives you that extra little bit of satisfaction."

"Always better, Aristo. There's nothing like complete ownership to remove those last little inhibitions."

"Unless you'd like to look over some of the Guiliano properties up for sale, you have plenty of time to visit the intake processing center here if you like - that's where your British trade-in is right now. I thought you might like to see the changes already in the slave," Aristo said. "As you know, a slave's first impression has a great deal to do with their success in training."

"You're right there," John replied. "But that Brit's going to be a handful, even though, as you said, you took that into account in estimating the trade-in value. But, in answer to your question, yes, I'd like to see your intake center. Guilo said he took the whole tour of your training facility and learned quite a bit as well as enjoying the scenery, as he put it. How about the whole tour?"

"It will take about four or five hours that I don't have right now, but Santos will be happy to show you around anytime you want. That way, you can arrange the transfer of funds, play around with those black slaves I'm having sent to your suite, screw your new Italian slave again, and tour the training facilities - all on your own schedule. Santos, as you know, was a trainer here and knows all the ends and outs of our training program. I'll notify them you're coming, but leave the time open. I'm having dinner around seven tonight and would love to have you join me along with two other potential buyers that are coming in later today. But if you want to eat in your suite, just let Santos know and he'll arrange it - anything you want can be prepared. The choice is up to you - charming company with yours truly or more time pleasuring yourself with those handsome blacks and Santos. Have Santos call me if you chose to have dinner over at my place."

"Who's coming to shop?" John asked. "Or is that confidential?"

"Here on the island, nothing needs to be confidential. After all, we're all into slaves or we wouldn't be here, would we? An American dealer from Houston specializing in imported foreign stock who claims he's interested in purchasing 20 to 30 to fill out his catalog if he can find the type of stock that sells well back in Texas and an oil sheik from Abu Dhabi whose looking for both jet blacks and blonds for his own household - that's the only type he's interested in buying. I've never dealt with them before so I have no idea of what they're like."

"Well, they could be interesting, Aristo. I give it some thought, depending on how tired I am after the tour."

Santos, sporting his shiny new collar and genital band, led the way to the intake center where, sure enough, the British slave was already well into his new life, although barely recognizable now that every bit of his facial and body hair had been shaved away, a heavy training collar had been installed along with two heavy iron tit rings and his genitals now projected obscenely due to a tight fitting genital band which had been welded on him. His prick and balls looked five times larger now that all the thick long pubic hair which partially hid them before had been removed and now that the genital banding positioned them prominently. The only thing remaining the same, at least for now, was the slave's heavy nose ring, not leashed at long last. Although his penis gag had been removed so he could now vocalize, a new, even larger butt plug had replaced his previous one, the new one featuring a pull ring that extended outside his anal opening so that the plug could be lodged deep inside him and yet still be easily retrievable when his trainers began their serious anal training procedures. When Santos pointed out the new arrival, it took John a few moments to realize it was the same person he had brought in a cage with him just hours ago. Currently, he was chained by his neck collar to a gang of about a dozen other slaves, obviously just as new to the experience as he was judging by faces filled with fear, their nervous twitching every time a whip cracked, and their instant screams of pain whenever the end of a trainer's whip tore into their flesh or the tip of an electric prod sizzled on some part of their totally accessible naked bodies.

"They've all been cleaned inside and outside, fitted for their training, and are ready to get their first meal now. They weren't fed during transit and so most of them haven't been fed for two or three days by now. At that level of hunger, a slave will do a lot of things without too much resistance they may have thought, up to now, they would never do. That's why the trainers will only allow them to eat after they have sucked off at least two other slaves in their lot and one of the trainers, including swallowing all three loads. If they won't do that, they just stay in place until they do."

"Anyone starve themselves to death, Santos?" John Morgan asked as he admired the selection of Guiliano stock - all of the slaves he saw were handsome, appealing, well built and well hung.

"No, master," Santos chuckled. "They say one held out for four days, but I never saw anyone over 36 hours myself. Hunger is a pretty powerful motivator, master. As they say, master, there are few martyrs among slaves."

"There are few martyrs anywhere when you get right down to it, Santos. Mostly the stuff of legends, I'm afraid."

"Yes, master. After swallowing a few loads of cum and then being fed, the initiates are then chained over those leather covered sawhorses you see over there and fucked by both the dildo master who uses a variety of shapes and sizes of dildos to forcefully fuck their hole and then, when well opened and fully lubricated, by one of the trainers who is especially well equipped to fully open them and to get them used to the real thing. Of course, master, most of the slaves have been raped long before this when they were first taken, or have been routinely fucked if they were bred to slavery, but we go through this procedure anyway so as to make every slave's experience equal. You can tell those new to anal usage - they're the ones screaming in pain and shock and choking in rage. The others you will notice are resigned to being fucked as part of their slavery and accept the fucking without comment or even, with some that are more sophisticated or those few naturally inclined to enjoy man to man sex, with enthusiasm. We don't gag a slave at this point - it's good to let them scream in protest - that way, they can see how fruitless it is - nothing changes. Your master wants to screw you - you get screwed. It's that simple and a slave has to learn that early on."

John looked around the huge room, paying special attention to those being screwed with either the super-sized dildos or by the well equipped trainers, obviously picked for this position with their penis size as an important criterion. Just as Santos had said, about half, tightly chained to the saw horses so their holes were totally accessible but yet fully restrained, were struggling and screaming and howling as their holes were assaulted by either plastic or the real thing. The other half were relatively silent outside of a few grunts and moans: some were passively accepting the inevitable with tears silently running down their cheeks; the other half were "into" it, bucking their restrained hips back toward the invading shaft synonymously with their user's insertions in order to assure full penetration with a glazed look of total satisfaction on their face. John shifted his eyes lower and, sure enough, this last group being fucked was fully erect and dripping copiously.

"We'll have to move on, master, if you want to see some of the other training facilities," Santos prompted subserviently. With a nod from his master, he led John Morgan to another huge room. "The slaves spend a good week getting used to sucking cock and being fucked. It's a lot easier for them when they see every other slave rapidly giving in to the demands of the trainers."

"Sort of like why fight it - it's inevitable anyway now that I'm a slave, Santos?"

"Exactly, master. That thought never escapes even the stupidest slave, master. In this room, a slave learns instant obedience to his new owner and to always work his hardest, no matter what the assignment. It's also where the slaves begin their serious physical conditioning so their bodies are fully developed to their maximum potential by the time they're auctioned off."

John saw the slaves here were fitted with shock collars and the tell-tale tiny antennas sticking out of their rumps told him the slaves had also been fitted with battery operated remote-controlled shock dildos as well. About 250 slaves were in the room, divided into small groups of eight, each with their own overseer. They were engaged in a complex and most demanding set of physical exercises that obviously taxed their bodies, wet with riverlets of sweat running down them and generally panting, if not heaving, for more air. The overseer's whips slashed into their backs and rumps to keep the pace up, and wild jerks and agonizing screams told John the remote control shocking devices were in heavy use. While they were watching the wild-eyed slaves trying desperately to keep up to the demands of their trainers, John saw three slaves faint dead away after a trainer had administered a particularly heavy shock to their collars, their screams of raw pain dying quickly away as they sunk to the floor. Another slave's agonizing scream led John to look in that direction: the slave was on his knees bent over into a fetal position as the electrified dildo within had obviously burnt some tissue - a tiny wiff of smoke was emanating from the slave's asshole.

But, as Santos pointed out, the rigorous training was paying off in two ways. All of the slaves were noticeably more physically developed and their muscles were almost "puffed" as the demanding routine perfected their potential. Most looked already like paragons of masculinity. Even more important, the slaves were learning to anticipate their trainer's commands in order to lessen their burden of pain. Now they worked up to maximum capacity without being told or waiting to be punished to act. Even better, now they obeyed instantly to any and all commands without waiting to see if they would be punished if they didn't. Furthermore, they even tried their best to anticipate what the trainers would want from them to minimize the punishments so readily available and so easily delivered. After a month in this room, Santos said as a given fact, slaves performed instantly and maximally no matter whether they were punished or not, or even if the instruments of punishment weren't there. Instant obedience and full capacity of response were habits now. Slaves no longer evaluated a command before responding - they just responded. They didn't even evaluate after a command had been fulfilled. As a slave, such an evaluation was pointless.

As a demonstration, Santos took one of the slaves under training and commanded him to pick up a nearby 100# sandbag and run full speed around the edge of the room until he was told to stop. The action had no purpose whatsoever other than to demonstrate the slave's abject obedience. The handsome, sweat soaked slave instantly complied with the command and performed the exhausting task until he looked ready to collapse and was gasping for air. Santos then told him to get on his hands and knees - he wanted to use his body as a bench. The slave instantly complied and as Santos' sat his full weight on the sweaty smooth back, placing one hand on the slave's butt and the other hand in the slave's hair, he scooted around a bit on the slave's broad back and then stuck two fingers of his right hand in the slave's mouth and two fingers of his left hand in the slave's asshole. As Santos' pumped the fingers in and out of the prospective holes, the slave never moved other than a muffled grunt as Santos inserted his long fingers all the way into the slave's body openings. Santos then stood up, wiped his fingers off in the slave's hair, and ordered the slave to a full display position, one of many slave positions learned in the initial stages of training. The slave instantly complied, still heaving from his exertions, but vainly trying to be absolutely still for the body inspection he anticipated. Santos reached down and stroked the sweaty shaft to a full erection and then churned the slave's balls vigorously, studying the slave's eyes for the slightest hint of resistance or rebellion. Seeing none, he ordered the slave to "position #3" where a well trained slave presents his asshole for inspection. The slave instantly complied and, grabbing the end of the implanted dildo, Santos dildo fucked the slave vigorously, again looking for any sign of resistance. When he slapped the slave on his butt brand as a sign he was through fucking him, the slave instantly resumed his standard display position with his eyes to the ground, humbly uttering a soft "Thank you, master," in acknowledgment of the special attention he had received.

"This slave is about ready for the next room I'll take you to, master. Would you like to examine the slave's manhood while he's displaying himself, master?" Santos asked.

John Morgan reached down and wrapped his fist around the still erect shaft of the trainee slave and stroked it a few times in admiration of its extreme girth. "Pretty as he is, he'd make a mistress awfully happy it would seem," he commented.

"Perhaps a wealthy woman will buy him for her pleasure," Santos agreed, "but this is the type that mainly appeals to the men customers, master, if I may say so."

The slave under discussion stared straight downward as he had been taught and had no reaction as to this scenario of his future life as the visitor proceeded to stroke his swollen shaft just short of an eruption, leaving him in gnawing need but knowing there was nothing he could do about it unless a trainer ordered it.

"Would you like to visit the sexual training room, master? That's where we learn to take the really big ones down our throat or up our ass, deliver a most satisfying fuck if our master or mistress so desires, and learn to best exhibit ourselves sexually, satisfy a sadist or even a masochist who might buy us, learn to keep ourselves hard for long periods when commanded to do so, and learn to produce multiple organism for demanding mistresses, masters who liked to be fucked themselves, or masters into milking their herd of slaves."

"Due to our time pressures, I just want to see the specific training where slaves learn to stay hard all the time and how slaves learn to produce load after load under command."

"Yes, master," Santos said as he headed his master back to a separate alcove off the main training room. "Basically, the slave's training starts by keeping him in a maximally erotic situation so he's hard to start with and it's easy to stay hard like these slaves here are constantly stroked by the trainers and kept hard continuously by never letting them unload. Then they make sure the slave has no opportunity to ever shoot off, even at night. They're kept shackled at night so they can't touch themselves and slaves in training like this are always kept in restraints so there is no way they can give each other relief - either with their hands or mouth or their ass. After a few weeks of this, their balls swell, but they're generally hard all the time. If a slave ever shoots off anyway without permission - like a wet dream or while being fucked - he's severely punished, so hard he'll never risk that again. By the end of the month, a slave is hard all the time and stays that way unless you dunk him in cold water or he gets sick. Usually, as an added touch, most slaves are dripping almost constantly by that time, master. Of course, you have to start with a slave that's easy to arouse to start with, but most slaves are due to their need."

"I want my team of black slaves to show hard all the time," John Morgan announced. "Do you think this Sergei will be able to arrange that? He's managed it with the Guiliano properties Count Parsimi has - those boys are hard around the clock it seems, even in hard labor."

"I'm sure this Sergei will accomplish the same thing with your own Guiliano properties, master. The procedure is relatively simple."

"Let's see the other training alcove - the one where slaves learn to deliver load after load on command."

"Yes, master. It's right over here." Santos said leading Mr. Morgan to the nearby area. "Basically, you start with good stud stock - stock you've noticed shoots off big thick loads several times a day, eliminating slaves that put out watery cum or slaves that shoot a big wad the first time and then very little the rest of the day. Taking the real studs, you then make their feed dependent on a good output of thick, rich cum. Each load produced meeting the specifications leads to getting a given amount of slave chow and a supplemental protein drink we recommend for slaves on a milking schedule. You never give a slave enough to live on until he's producing at least six to eight loads of at least a half-cup each time every day. You leave it up to the slave after that - whatever imagery he has to have, whatever experiences he has to relive in his mind, whatever turns him on - that's up to the slave. But he's got to realize he won't be fed unless he produces. Nobody's going to feed a dried up cow. Within a week, they've lost a few pounds but they're got the hang of it. When that happens, they generally can get it up to a minimum of eight times a day, sometimes ten, and with all that food and protein drink coming in, they quickly gain back any weight they lost. Slaves trained like this have two markets: milk studs for owners who like a fresh supply of thick, hot cum as a dietary supplement, a tonic, a youth elixir, or condiment sauce at their table; or as a practically inexhaustible stud for a mistress or master who likes to have the slave ejaculate each time they are called into action for added realism. Of course, most mistresses and masters wanting a slave to fuck them for their enjoyment usually command the slave not to orgasm so the slave can keep fucking indefinitely. I've been used by several mistresses coming to the island to buy slaves who have used me in that fashion, master."

"What fashion, Santos? Shooting off over and over, or being ordered to not orgasm at all?"

"Being ordered to control myself properly, master," Santos smiled.

"That's more like it in my opinion. No reason a properly trained slave shouldn't be able to control his body as ordered."

"Of course, master," Santos agreed.

"The last room, Master, you should see on your visit is the sales preparation room, which is only open until 4 PM so we'll need to hurry. It's the final stage of the Guiliano training program and teaches the slave how to find a new owner. Every slave at this stage knows if he doesn't attract an owner within a reasonable time of being put up for sale, he'll either be sent back for another round of training or sold off to a wholesaler where they're most likely to end up as draft slaves in the mines or in manufacturing plants where life is harsh and often brief under a heavy whip."

"If they know that, it looks like you would get upmost cooperation from the slaves in teaching them what they need to know," John Morgan smiled. "I've seen slaves down in the mines."

"Yes, master. Some slaves here were placed in manufacturing plants before they were lucky enough to be bought by a Guiliano agent and sent here. They're very easy to train because they claim anything is better than where they came from - most cooperative, they are, master."

"Well, I would think," John Morgan responded.

By then, they were in a large airy room where hundreds of well-honed naked bodies were busily applying body oils, shaving themselves, plucking out hairs from below their gonads and from their arm pits and from around their ringed nipples. Others were practicing poses of various types under glaring lights while their trainers stood to one side commanding them to turn a little this way, thrust their pelvis out a little more, tilt their head a little to one side, etc. Still others were in one display position or another as their trainers roughly handled their bodies everywhere imaginable to acclimate the slaves to constant fondling and minute examination during the buying process. Some were having their balls roughly massaged until the slaves groaned and bit their lips, but never made an attempt to pull away or withdraw; others were having their penises stroked until they were raw and abraded, even bleeding a little, but again, none pulled away or did anything but smile as their trainers abused them. Still others were bent over as trainers roughly shoved their fingers, large dildos, even fists, up their lubricated assholes. Again the slaves groaned, moaned, and even silently cried as their ass chutes were ravished to the point of bleeding, but none moved from position, none cried out in protest, and all just smiled no matter what was being done to them. At another place, some slaves had bleeding nipples from the nibbling and biting of their ringed tits by the trainers. The trainees' tits were red and angry from the abuse, but the slaves never did anything but thrust their nipples into the hands and mouths of the very trainers that were abusing them. Instead of screaming in agony, they cried silently, bit their lips, and smiled at their abuser.

"A slave has to learn he's going to be tested thoroughly in the sales room," Santos commented, "and some of those tests are going to be painful. But, if you want to get sold, a slave has to learn some sacrifices are necessary usually."

"Even if a sadist buys you and bites your nipples clear off?" John Morgan asked, almost to himself.

"A slave has no choice of who he is sold to, master," Santos said without emotion. "But if he is sold to such a person, he must realize he is just a piece of meat like any other livestock and is, in fact, a piece of property to be done with as his master or mistress sees fit."

"Still, Santos," John Morgan argued, "a slave must have some feelings left in him, despite all the training."

Santos smiled and said, "A smart slave can shape his master to a slight extent, master. Perhaps a little honey given the master now and then will soften the most harsh owner, master."

"What does that mean, Santos?" John scoffed.

"If I do my best and make your life as pleasant and enjoyable as possible, maybe you won't be so harsh with your property?" Santos suggested.

"Fine in many cases, but some owners might turn out to be true sadists where the pleasant and enjoyable you are talking about is simply torturing the slave."

"In that case, master, a slave has no choice but to endure the situation the best he can. He has no other alternative. The best lesson a slave can learn is he or she has practically no alternatives from now on - his life is pretty well determined by whoever buys him and what they want."

"A lesson well learned. I suppose, in the final analysis, that's exactly what these slaves here are learning as they prepare for the sales room. Make themselves as appealing as possible and accept whatever happens."

"Exactly, master. If I may say so without offending you, master, I admire your sharp intellect and considerable insight into slavery. How lucky I am to be owned by you."

"You whore, you. Trying to sugar mouth me already. Don't you think if I'm so damn smart and insightful, as you claim, I'm immune to all the bullshit that comes out of your mouth," John Morgan said with a snicker.

"Yes, master," Santos said. "Shall we go back to your apartment so you can fuck me again or would you prefer the two blacks first or, perhaps, a nice afternoon suck?"

"All of the above, Santos, and, as I just said, you're a real whore you know."

"Yes, master," Santos said with a very broad smile himself, his own huge sex swelling in anticipation of the coming events.

John Morgan had Santos suck both black slaves off for his amusement and then had Santos call Aristo Mythos to confirm the dinner appointment before fucking first Santos and then one of the black slaves before showering and dressing for dinner.

The Texas slave dealer turned out to be a huge bore and instead of a being a connoisseur of exotic foreign imports, reminded you of a cattle dealer who bought and sold stock by the pound. It was obvious he was only interested in the cheapest stock - those only capable of moving in response to a cattle prod or a heavy whip. John Morgan realized instantly the Texan would probably buy nothing but complain about the high prices before he moved on.

Aristo was barely civil to the uncouth Texan and whispered "cowboy" in John's ear at one point during the dinner. When the Texan claimed he always had "hot sauce" with his "veggies," and stroked every single one of the slave waiters until they shot off right onto his plate which he then dipped his food in and swallowed with great flourish and a lot of talk about "real men on the range," and so forth, Aristo had had all he could take.

"My slave you just masturbated without my permission is particularly good in his sucking skills. If you take him right now to your quarters you can have him for the night. Otherwise, I'm afraid all the slaves have other assigned duties.

"Yahoo, Mr. Greekman or I'll nickname you 'My-thee' since you seem kind of girly like. I'll just take you up on that offer, My-thee-boy, because that there slave has one hell of a prick on him, almost as big as a good Texas prick. When he swallows the likes of me, it may stretch his throat to breaking - just warning you, My-thee, in that I doubt if he's been put to a real man before."

"Just take him," Aristo said icily. "When will you be leaving? I'm afraid we can't get you back to your Delos connection any time but early in the morning. Our schedule simply won't allow any other times. Six AM?"

"Jesus Christ, My-thee. Get all the way over here and barely have time to look at your overpriced stock. Well, hell, I haven't seen much I could sell back in Texas anyway. We're looking for value when we buy a piece of livestock."

"The staff will pick you up at 6 AM then for your return to Delos," Mythos said coldly. "Just leave my slave in the room. We'll pick him up later."

"What's left of the dumb bastard, My-thee. Looks like I won't have anything else to do but fuck the shit out of him all night long. Can't I even spend some time looking over the caged stock in the sales room?"

"No, that's not possible. We close the sales room after 5 PM in that our stock has to be fully rested and cleaned up thoroughly for examination the coming day."

"Well, how about another one of these slave waiters, My-thee. It's kind of boring with just one to plug all night."

"The others have other assignments," Aristo said in finality. "The slave I've loaned you will show you back to your guest suite."

"Yeah...Yeah...I know a brush-off when I get it...." the Texas dealer grumbled as he grabbed the loaned slave by his dick and roughly yanked him out of the room.

"You handled the lout beautifully, Aristo," the other guest, a handsome sheik from the U.A.E. commented. "Remind me never to go near Texas, although I almost pitied the poor slave assigned to his suite tonight."

"Well, that's a slave's lot, Sheik Tarig, although I share your thought."

"Sheik Tarig, have you had a chance yet to examine any of the Guiliano slaves?" I asked.

"Yes and no, Mr. Morgan," he said charmingly, his good looks almost distracting. "I own three Guiliano boys already but I didn't purchase them here, but from owners who had originally purchased them here. But I have been able to visit the sales room for a few hours this afternoon and, frankly, I've seen enough to know I'm going to buy more than I originally thought." He smiled at Aristo. "Assuming, of course, that the most hospitable Mr. Mythos is willing to sell me some of his obviously well trained and highly selective stock. I think you will find, Mr. Mythos, that if I find what I want, I generally won't haggle over the price. Quality speaks for itself, as the Texan so aptly illustrated he has so little of."

His subtle humor, combined with his charming directness, instantly drew Mr. Morgan to him.

"Mr. Morgan here just bought nine slaves today: eight a matched team of well-built mulattoos - half Mandingo black, half French all from the same stud - and one of my long-time slave trainers, an Italian slave that's very easy on the eye. It's my understanding he's going to use the black slaves for some new contraption to get him around his estate called a 'slavemobile.'"

"Slavemobile? That sound's interesting. Exactly what is it?" Sheik Tarig chuckled.

"Sort of like a fancy golf cart up front powered by six slaves in the rear chained to a treadmill basically. I liked the novelty of it," John Morgan replied. "I wanted the six slaves to be essentially black, good looking, muscular, and closely matched in size, color, and sexual equipment for a good display. Aristo here found me eight slaves fitting the bill and extremely well matched, so I bought a couple of spares while I had the chance."

"And you bought one of Guiliano's trainers to handle them?" the Sheik continued.

"Not really," John laughed. "I bought the Italian for a good friend of mine, Count Parsimi in Italy, who's been eager to get his hands on him ever since he bedded the slave down right here some time ago on a buying trip. Actually, I've giving him the slave on a long-term loan in exchange for his slave handler, a Polish slave, who I know will whip my black team into shape in no time at all."

"And this Polish slave of the Count's, will he be useful in other ways?" the Sheik asked with an arched eyebrow.

"Very useful," John smiled. "He's extremely good looking, very well trained, and magnificently equipped for a white slave."

"Yes, I have found Poles an interesting breed. They are either as you describe this handler you're taking on loan or just big brutes sold fairly cheaply as draft slaves. I have two Polish slaves at my own compound - both are blonds, extremely handsome, well equipped and eager to please. I keep their bodies completely shaved below the neck, but I like their fine head hair so well I've let it grow out full length. One of them has hair flowing down past his shoulders now."

"I take it their training extends to their bed manners?" John Morgan asked.

"Of course, Mr. Morgan. At first, they seemed a little hesitant - the handler told me they had little experience other than a few farm girls before they were enslaved - but that's not to say they were uncooperative or anything - they were far too well trained for that. More like shy and inhibited, I suppose, but they soon got over that and now seem to thoroughly enjoy being selected for use. Of course, it's the only outlet they're ever allowed, so I suppose that has something to do with it." Chuckling at the thought, he added, "I know that would have a strong effect on me in a short period of time."

"How old were they when you bought them, Sheik Tariq," I asked. "I understand age of entry has a lot to do with it," John added.

"Around 18 or 19, I believe, Mr. Morgan. I rarely buy slaves much older than that - previous habits are hard to break sometimes."

"My point exactly, Sheik," John smiled. "I can see our experiences in slave ownership have taught us the same things despite the great distance between our homes."

"Yes, John, if I may be so personal as to call you by your first name. Slaves are universal around the world despite their origins. Once properly trained, they pretty well react all the same to their slavery, especially if they're introduced to it during the formulative years. A person enslaved later in life, in their late 40s or 50s generally has a struggle accepting his new status and, in my opinion, isn't worth the training time involved."

"Sheik Tariq," John started.

"Hammad, please, John," the Sheik smiled warmly.

"Hammad, you don't look much over 20 or so, but you're obviously wise beyond your years. Me, I didn't understand these things until I was 30 or so and even now, at 32, feel naive about slavery sometimes. But you seemed to grasp the whole concept so well. I've owned slaves over the years from central Africa, the U.S., South America, Cambodia, India, and Romania to name just a few. No matter where they came from originally, within a few months they're more or less the same outside of the way they look. You're precisely right - they all react the same to their slavery, as you so well put it."

"John, I'm 21 for your information. Younger than a lot of my slaves, not that it matters. But I'm afraid I have an unfair advantage on you, John. You see, I grew up in a society where slavery has always been widely practiced since time immemorial - understanding slaves is just something you grow up with. It's just that I'm more fortunate than most in my country - I'm able to buy as many as I want, although even some of the working poor have at least one or two of the cheaper type of slaves to help them around the house and fulfill their sexual needs. In your country, only a very few of the wealthiest elite even know slavery still exists and thrives, let alone are able to buy slaves for themselves. It's two quite different upbringings."

"You've precisely described my original predicament, Hammad. I was 25 before I even found out slaves still existed and 27 before I figured out how to buy one. As Aristo here will testify, I didn't even make it to Guiliano's here until I was 28, when I made my very first purchases abroad."

"And good ones they were as I recall," Aristo joined the conversation. "A couple of blacks from the States phenomenally hung, a beautiful 19-year-old blond from Germany, and a handsome boy from Algeria who was built like a bull, bought out of a brothel, and was hard all the time."

"What a memory," John exclaimed in amazement. "I'd practically forgotten about that Algerian boy myself."

"A memory like a databank," Sheik Tariq added. "Phenomenal."

"What happened to those four, John?" Aristo asked. "You don't still have them, do you?"

"The blacks are still with me - they're two of the four I mentioned I've got at home. They're a lot older but wiser now, but they're better in bed than they ever were - that's why I keep them around. My guests love them so they're kept pretty busy. But you had them well trained, so I've never had any real trouble with them and they seem to like their life on the estate pretty well. Been offered a pretty penny for them by some guests who were pretty impressed when they bedded them down, but I've resisted selling them so far regardless of what I'm offered."

"How old are they now?" Aristo asked. "Around 24 or so?"

"That sounds about right. They were 19 when I bought them and you'd had them a year in training so I suppose they were 18 or so when you bought them off that Texas detention center you had some connection with."

"Well, they're good for another 15 to 20 years doing just what they're doing if you keep them exercised and fed right," Aristo said assuredly. "We've found American blacks hold up well even under very heavy usage. That's why they have great resale value if you ever want to sell them."

"Thanks for the tip, Aristo," John said. "Before you ask, the German got his butt sold to a business partner I had from Saudi Arabia who just got obsessed with the boy's goodies. He paid me a cool one million U.S. to take him back to Jeddah with him. Let's see, that was in 2006, and he was going to stud the slave as well as have him serve as his chauffeur and valet. I imagine by now that blond beauty has produced at least a couple of dozen new slaves in the making that probably will end up in the local markets at a good price. The dusky boy from Algeria didn't work out too well. We just couldn't keep him busy enough at the estate: he was like a dog in heat always trying to jerk himself off, or trying to hump one of the other slaves the minute he wasn't being watched, and dripping all over the place with cum oozing out of that big prick of his, including on some of my most expensive Turkish rugs. I got tired of it and sold him to a male brothel in London - a brothel was where he came from to start with. To make a long story short, the slave was delighted with his new home where he would have an endless stream of customers day and night, the brothel buying him particularly wanted a Middle-

Eastern type to add to their line-up, and I was happy with the 450,000 pounds sterling they paid me for him."

"Slavery has a way of letting everyone seek out their destiny," Sheik Tarig commented. "In my religion, it's clear evidence of Allah's will. Inshallah!"

"You got an excellent price for the Algerian boy, John," Aristo complimented John. "That London brothel worked him hard, I'm sure. Unfortunately, boys in brothels don't last long these days and so you have to get your money's worth out of them up front. Disease is such a problem now among the lower classes who patronize the brothels, not having the means to buy even the ugliest slave for their own use. I wouldn't step foot into an brothel open to the public these days."

At that point, the two remaining slaves serving as waiters brought an ice cream sundae as dessert and placed the dishes in front of each of the three diners. The thick sauce on top of the walnut ice cream was warm and melted the ice cream underneath it rapidly.

"This dessert is a specialty of the house," Aristo said as he lifted his spoon in invitation to partake. "I'm sure you'll enjoy the unique flavor."

Both John and the Sheik instantly recognized the sauce and appreciated its creamy texture and tangy taste, but mixed with the walnut ice cream added a new taste sensation.

"Delicious," Sheik Tariq said. "The cum sauce brings out the flavor of the ice cream beautifully. Is the sauce from these slaves?" he asked, looking up at the naked waiters standing at full display.

"Yes, even though with that uncouth Texan I didn't know if we'd have enough left for dessert," Aristo laughed. "But it seems the slave's balls filled up fast enough."

The guests quickly finished the gourmet treat scooping their dish to get the last drop before finishing.

"Another helping?" Aristo asked. "One scoop hardly seems enough." The waiters, hearing this, tensed in anticipation and their pricks began to swell to full erection in readiness. "See, the waiters are interested in serving another round, pointing to their full erections."

"No, thank you," both John and Sheik Tariq answered at once. "We have to watch our waistline," Hammad explained while John nodded in agreement. "But I'll remember and try it at home

- black walnut ice cream topped with warm cum - a very nice combination."

"If I could be so bold, Sheik Tariq, could I arrange for a couple of slaves I think you would like to be delivered to your suite this evening? John here is already taken care of - a couple of blacks he liked that helped him out of the yacht and his new purchase, the Italian slave I mentioned."

"It would be appreciated, Aristo. Usually, I travel with a selection of my own slaves, but I didn't bother for an overnight stay and I was, frankly, hoping you've loan me a slave or so for my bed this evening. I was going to inquire about the possibility of an overnight loan but you've most graciously beat me to the punch."

"I'm aware you prefer light-skinned blonds and very dark blacks, so I've been presumptuous enough to arrange one of each to be delivered to your suite about now as well as a most unusual slave I thought you might enjoy as well," Aristo announced.

"Unusual, Aristo? How? And don't tell me to wait and see. I'm not that patient, although your generosity is impressive and certainly appreciated," the Sheik replied.

"The first slave is a Romanian, 20-years-old, muscular, handsome as they come, and the epitome of manhood between his legs. He's got long blond hair but the rest of his body is shaved so show off his flawless white skin, tanned just a bit to show well. The second slave is from the Sudan, shiny jet black with close cut kinky black hair and a hairless body. He's 6'4", built like a bull, phenomenally hung, but has the face of an angel set off my most unusual green eyes. He's 20 also as I recall. The third slave, the surprise, is a handsome very dark brown boy, almost black, with pure blond hair, blue eyes, creamy smooth skin, and magnificently built. The blond hair comes from his mother, a big Swede owned by a breeding farm in North Africa who uses a strikingly handsome huge black Hausa from central Africa as the house stud. As I'm sure you're aware, Sheik, the Hausa men, along with Mandingos, have always been the choice of black slaves among discriminating buyers. This particular offspring has the color and body build of his sire with the hair and eyes of his brood. Best of all, he's like most Hausas - hot and ready to go all the time and simply inexhaustible sexually. But let me warn you, Sheik Tariq, this slave has a monstrous prick - way too big to ever let him fuck anything as he'd tear it up - so he's usually hard and dripping all the time. The trainers told me to milk him right off the bat so he calms down a little before bedding him. I followed their advice and it worked out fine so I'm passing the little hint on. That boy spews out a good cup or so of juice when he is milked, so be prepared!"

"Most interesting, Aristo. All three sound interesting, but the last one sounds like he might make a good milk stud," Sheik Tariq answered, licking his lips a little.

"That he would, but he's too valuable for just that. Once he's calmed, he'll take a fuck like you won't believe - I think it's his ass muscles or something - and his cocksucking skills are unsurpassed. Be prepared - the slave can leave you totally exhausted, Hammad. At least he does me."

"Do I detect some preliminary sales routine?" Sheik Tariq laughed. "From your description of the slaves you're loaning me tonight, it sounds like I should buy them and not bother to look at the others."

"May well be, Sheik, but we've got plenty of others I think you'll like as well," Aristo assured the young buyer.

The Texan lummox was long gone by the time Aristo Mythos, Sheik Tariq, and John Morgan had breakfast together. All had a look of total satiation and a touch of weariness from the night's activities.

"Just coffee," Aristo told the naked waiter. Smiling at the other two, he admitted, "I've already had a most delicious morning snack," nodding at one of the freshly assigned waiters, a handsome young Latino whose long, thick penis, now only semi-erect and still shiny from saliva, as well as his flushed skin was a sure sign he'd recently been completely drained. "We Greeks believe a youth's cum has anti-aging properties, but, whether it does or not, I find it a most satisfying breakfast."

"Crispy bacon and three eggs sunny side up for me," John ordered. "I'm starved."

"Fruit and coffee with rolls," the Sheik ordered.

As the three waiters scurried away, freshly scrubbed and body shaved, the three men smiled at each other as they watched the waiter's tight butts churn around their deeply embedded butt plugs as they walked away.

"I'll buy all three," Sheik Tariq smiled at Aristo.

"I assume you don't mean the three waiters?" Aristo chuckled.

"No, Aristo. The three sent to my suite during dinner last night. I assume their price is fair."

"Most competitive, Sheik," Aristo assured him. "As I recall, those three will run you approximately 1.6 million euros, but I'll check to be sure when I get a chance. It's on the computer. Would you like to look at some others?"

"Seems reasonable, considering the quality," the Sheik commented casually as if spending 1.6 million euros was an everyday occurrence. "I can have the funds transferred almost instantly from my bank in Dubai. But I would like to look at some others."

"You want to shop around a bit more, or are you ready to take off, John? I have all the ownership papers, receipts, certificates of health, passports, provenances, and so forth all ready right here if you'll like to look them over. Your payment came through fine. Guiliano Imports wants to thank you for your business, John, as usual."

"Santos said there's a American slave I should look at before I leave," John Morgan said. "That whore is your best salesman, Aristo," he added. "He came up with that suggestion just as I had shot another load down his throat and he was cleaning me. Claimed he had trained the American himself and, once I saw him, I'll probably want to buy him. You're right, Aristo, you should have clipped his vocal chords years ago," he laughed.

"Well, if I had I might have lost a sale," Aristo chuckled in return. "I know the one he's talking about and, I hate to tell you, John, but Santos is right. You'll get a hard on just looking at him - he's just your type."

"Sounds like we'll be shopping together after all, John," Sheik Tariq interjected. "I'd like nothing better. Perhaps we could swap notes on how best to assess the commodities being offered today."

"I imagine my techniques are the same as yours, Hammad. You're decisive, I see, especially after sampling the goods overnight."

"Yes, how do you English put it so well, 'the proof is in the pudding?'"

"Testing them out is always good, but sometimes not always possible in some markets," John said. "Here at Guiliano's, they always let you thoroughly examine a slave before purchasing, including having them service you completely if you so desire."

The slave waiters returned with the breakfast orders which were quickly disposed of. Sheik Hammad seemed interested in one of the waiters, a blond Russian boy so pretty he would look feminine if it wasn't for his heavy musculature and huge sexual organs. He reached up and, firmly gripping the slave's organ, quickly stroked him to a full erection. The slave looked pleased at the attention given him and subtly thrust his organ even further into the guest's hand. The Sheik then had the slave get on his knees with his hands behind his collared neck so that his tits and chest development, as well as his almost delicate face, could be explored.

"How much, Aristo?" the Sheik asked with mild interest.

"It's a bargain, Sheik. Russians have flooded the market recently and prices are depressed for boys like this: 185,000 euros and he's yours, fully trained and just turned 19. He took to his training so well it only took him five months to reach our standards and the trainers tell me he's frisky as a hungry pup in bed, no matter what you have in mind."

"I'm afraid I'm not familiar with the word 'frisky,' Aristo. What does it mean?"

"It means he's eager as all get out to please you anyway you want any time, Sheik."

"The price is a pittance - are you sure there's nothing wrong with the property?"

"Not a thing, Sheik. It's just young blond Russians like him are a dime a dozen right now. A few years from now, I predict his appreciated value will be something like 300,000 to 400,000 euros and you can enjoy him in the interim. Properties like this should be viewed as a good long-term investment right now - beats money in the bank at current interest rates."

"You're very convincing, Aristo. I'll take him, but I still want to look at the others."

The slave just sold looked overjoyed. His long waiting time in the crowded sales pens (along with the endless body inspections) was over and he was definitely sexually aroused by his new owner's youth and good looks. Fate had smiled on him, at least until he was sold off again when he had appreciated in value and his new owner could make a handsome profit off of his investment.

"Quick and decisive," John Morgan commented on the sale. "As I said before, I like that in a man, Hammad. I'm sure that trait serves you well in other aspects of the business world."

"What other aspects, John?" the Sheik asked without malice. "My family's wealth allows me freedom to do what I want, but, as it turns out, I am good in what I do. You see, John, my family's wealth can easily be traced to the slave trade. We've been the leading slave merchants in my country for centuries and it seems to be in my blood. My modest dealings to date, although I was still a minor at the time, have proven to be most profitable for the family and they are urging me, now that I am finally of age, to expand my hobby into a full time occupation similar to my father and grandfather and great grandfather before me."

"A competitor to Guiliano Imports?" Aristo laughed. "That's fine - we like competition. Keeps us on our toes. And, as you will learn once you really get into the business, we trade our stock around with our main competitors quite a bit. Gives us variety and helps us get rid of surplus in certain categories we've overbought in for one reason or another."

"Makes sense, Aristo. I'll remember that. The markets in my country get so loaded up with black slaves and have trouble meeting demand for whites - we need to ship you excess blacks in exchange for your white stock that isn't selling - like this Russian slave I just purchased at a depressed price. In Dubai, I could sell him tomorrow for 300,000 U.S. dollars and when he's fleshed out with maturity and more experience, he'd bring 500,000 U.S. On the other hand, you can buy a beautiful black for a mere 100,000 euros or so in Dubai - there's just too many available right now. I blame the breeding farms springing up all over, but others say it's due to the endless civil wars in Africa. Whoever wins always wants to sell their prisoners for whatever they can get for them at the nearest market. They always need ready cash to buy more guns to stay in power. Sudanese slaves are selling as low as $10,000 at some local markets and that's for a full grown man whose decent looking and trained to obedience."

The three men proceeded immediately to the sales room following their breakfast. Aristo's new handler, Santos' replacement, had the presentations well organized since Aristo had already alerted him as to the two customers' preferences. Sheik Tariq ended up buying nine more fine-looking Russian blonds, similar to the waiter he had bought earlier. Although varying considerably in height and the composition of their facial features, they were all trim but heavily muscled, completely body shaved, and, like all Guiliano stock seemingly, very well hung. As usual, the decision to purchase was made quickly without reservations just as soon as he had checked each for genital arousal and tightness of their anal chutes. The Sheik ordered each of them, along with his earlier purchase, be genitally banded to guarantee excellent display, tit ringed, and fitted with a tall collar that would force their heads into a chronic upright position.

John suggested he examine the four blacks he had so enjoyed in his suite. "They're about as eager to please as any slaves I've seen," John said, "and I can guarantee their stamina," he added with a smirk.

"I'm sure they're excellent, John, but, as I said, our local market is just gutted with blacks currently. I'll lose money on them at what I'm sure Guiliano would have to charge me."

"Not necessarily," Aristo interposed. "We got them dirt cheap ourselves at a clearance sale in Miami, Florida. They were construction workers picking up a little extra hustling the streets. Their foreman got wind of their extracurricular activities, knew they didn't have any family, and sold them to one of our agents at bargain basement prices. Of course, we've had the expense of training them and feeding them for some time - they took a while to get fully trained. Their foreman invited them over for a beer after work one day and slipped them a knock-out drug. When they woke up, they were here in a cage butt naked with a collar around their necks," he laughed.

"Americans? How much for the four of them before I decide whether it's worth my time to even look them over," Sheik Tariq said languidly.

"We've had them around a while and they're not selling, Sheik. I'd like to get rid of them. How about a special price of 45,000 euro each if you buy all four as a lot or 55,000 for just one of them. That's a lot more than you could pay for a black slave in their prime in Dubai, I know, but these boys are perfectly trained. And, as John says, they're a wonder in bed. I've used them a few times myself and I certainly agree with John."

"170,000 for the lot, Aristo. Otherwise, I have no chance of ever getting my money out of them, let alone a profit. As it is, my only hope to dispose of them would be with a foreign buyer visiting our markets who is unaware of local prices on blacks."

Aristo pondered the proposal for a good minute before ordering the handler to get the four American blacks out of their cages and up on the sales platform for inspection.

Sheik Tariq hefted the four sets of balls, stroked each to a quick erection, and had each bend over to inspect his hole, all within a few minutes. "Very well, Aristo, 170,000 euros for the lot?"

"Sold," Aristo said with a smile. "How do you want them fitted, Sheik? Just like the Russian purchases?

"No, Aristo. For these, I want a heavy bronze collar with leash rings on all sides, larger 2" tit rings in bronze, a 1-1/2" genital band to make sure they protrude out as far as possible, and, for these blacks, I think a 2" nose ring right through the septum would make them more interesting looking. That way they can be led around ring-leashed by their nose, something they never would have dreamed of in their previous life in Miami. It will serve as a constant reminder that now they are just an animal."

"Oh, I think they already know that," John laughed. "Wait until you bed them down and you'll see what I'm talking about."

"I'd like to look at a Greek boy whose small but muscular with dark hair and blue eyes if you have one on hand," Sheik Tariq inquired. "My cousin has been looking for some months now but hasn't found anything locally, but, Aristo, he wants one extraordinarily equipped - he's got a - what to you English call it - a 'fetish' about that aspect of a slave."

Aristo checked his hand held computer and soon ordered the handler to bring the contents of Cages #1101 and #47 for inspection. While waiting for the delivery, Aristo said one of those being brought up for examination was Greek and the other was a Macedonian, if that made any difference.

"I doubt it," Sheik Tariq laughed. "My cousin is so stupid he wouldn't even know the two countries are different. He's more interested in looks than substance."

The handler quickly arrived with the two offerings who promptly assumed the full display position on the sales platform while the handler again dropped to his knees with his head bowed to one side. Both properties were exactly as requested: black hair, blue eyes, small in frame but not in musculature, and practically freakish between their legs as the long tubes, too heavy for full erection, swung down almost to their knees. But one was considerably more handsome than the other with his long eye lashes, a cute smile with dimples, and sparkling eyes.

"Which is the Greek?" Aristo teased.

"The slave on the right," Sheik Tariq said promptly, pointing to the handsome one.

"How did you know, Sheik?" Aristo questioned with considerable admiration in his voice.

"No Macedonian has eyelashes like a woman," Sheik Tariq answered quickly. "The Greek boy would make a good-looking woman if his body was completely covered. I'll buy him if the price is reasonable."

"He's small so he's discounted, Sheik. 105,000 U.S. dollars is what we're asking That's less than 90,000 in euros. Small slaves just don't bring as much."

"Well, he's certainly not small down here," Sheik Aristo said as he lifted the huge organ in the palm of his hand and sort of patted it until it began to swell significantly and the slave flushed slightly in his arousal as he tilted his pelvis upward for his inspector's convenience in handling him. As soon as the organ was fully aroused, Sheik Aristo announced, "I'll take him at the price you mentioned. My cousin will love him as a birthday gift, but it's some time before the birthday rolls around. In the interim, he could prove most interesting in my own bed. A small slave is always more fun to fuck in my opinion. Their holes are usually so tight; it's fun to see the slave struggle to accommodate a good stretching of their chute. I want him fitted with only a tight fitting slave collar and he'll need a real thick genital band with that monster, both in copper with his skin coloring. I want leash rings attached to both his collar and his band."

The Macedonian slave looked dejected, knowing he might spend weeks more cramped in a tiny cage awaiting another potential buyer. There, with his hands cuffed behind his back, his head bent over by the cage roof above him, and forced to sit on his rump as the only possible position, he would be forced to literally sit and stare at the huge tool between his legs day after day, dripping in constant need. The Greek slave was excited at finally attracting a buyer, but the last comment of his new owner clearly indicated he was to serve as a bed buck for a strangely dressed man in a far away land and then be given away as a gift to some relative of him with the same usage intended. But, he reflected, that's what he had been trained to do all these months, and it certainly beat sitting in a cage week after week completely restrained except for the daily exercise routines.

"That's 18 purchases by my tally, Aristo," the Sheik said. "That's it for me so figure up the total and I'll have the funds transferred immediately so I can be on my way. With this many, have them all cleansed inside and out, plugged and caged for a chartered air transport. Add that to the bill while you're at it, Aristo."

Aristo fiddled with his Palm Pilot a bit and then gave the Sheik the total cost as well as the shipping charges with a discrete air charter service Guiliano Imports recommended for safe, rapid, and totally discrete delivery. "If you just poke in your bank account number, Sheik and push enter so it's totally confidential, I can get the funds transferred right now to cover the whole amount."

The Sheik quickly entered his secret 10-digit number and, almost instantly, the transfer was made to the Guiliano Import account.

"Loved doing business with you, Sheik Tariq. One of many future transactions I hope. When you get home and look over your inventory, give me a call and we can work out some transfers of overstocks to both our advantages," he suggested.

"That's exactly what I intend to do," Sheik Tariq said. "I only deal in quality stock, as you know, and it's obvious that's your intent also judging from what I've seen today. That will make transferring surplus stocks easy without a lot of hassle."

"Exactly what I had in mind," Aristo said as he smiled broadly.

"Well, John, see anything you're interested in?" Aristo asked. "I suppose you haven't had a chance with the Sheik buying. I'll get that American Santos mentioned up here for your inspection before I forget it. He's quite something to look at whether you buy him or not."

The handler delivered the American slave under discussion within minutes. He was, as Aristo had said, simply breathtaking. Light tan, he had sandy hair in a shag cut, piercing brown eyes marked by long black eyelashes and dark eyebrows, high cheekbones, a small mouth, a straight narrow nose, a neatly trimmed black mustache with a matching pencil line beard outlining his square jaws and chin. His body was shaved clean, but it was obvious he had little body hair anyway. Thus, every muscle was outlined, and his body resembled a Greek statue in polished tan marble with one exception - his flaccid genitals were beautiful shaped but about four times larger than any Greek statue.

John Morgan was stunned by the beauty of the naked man standing quietly in front of him in the classic display position with an inviting smile on his face. "An American? But from where?" John finally asked after he had taken the entire body in.

"A Kansas farm boy originally. Orphaned at 13 and sent to a large residential foster home run by a private corporation in Topeka that takes the best looking of their charges and grooms them for overseas sales. Our agent in Topeka is actually the head social worker that runs the place. He makes sure his sales can never be traced and it has proven quite profitable to him over the years. We've had a number of Kansas boys trained and then sold here because of the connection. This one is 19 now, totally acclimated to his new status as a slave, and fully trained to please even the most discerning master or mistress. But, because of his looks, he's a little on the high side, John."

John reached out and, taking the boy's huge tool in his hand, began stroking it. The boy quickly became aroused and even started bucking in John's hand a little as he pleadingly looked at the prospective purchaser.

"Please buy me, master," the boy whispered, audible only to the man examining his sex.

John's other hand hefted the ball sac and weighed it, then squeezed and pinched the boy's big juicy tits, rubbed his pecs to ascertain the degree of musculature there and finally inserted a finger in the boy's mouth which was promptly swallowed and sucked deep into his mouth while the slave's tongue massaged the inserted finger. Once the boy started dripping pre-cum as a result of being stroked vigorously, John motioned for the slave to turn around and, after checking out his back muscles and examining his Guiliano brand on the butt cheek, took his hand to the boy's head and bent him over to test out his hole. Immediately the handler arrived with a cart filled with greased dildos. John selected a big one - the 12 x 6" model popular in slave sales auctions, and unceremoniously rammed it up the slave's proffered hole. The boy groaned as he wiggled his ass to try to accommodate the invasion, but soon, with a few more gasps and groans, the dildo was all the way up the boy's hole with only a tiny tear spilling down one cheek as the slave adjusted to the pain. Completely trained, the boy turned his handsome head back and smiled invitingly despite the pain he was obviously experiencing to indicate his total subservience to the wishes of a master. John began pumping the huge dildo in and out of the boy to study his reaction to a deep fucking. The boy accepted what was being done to his body with little resistance or remorse. Instead, he seemed worried that he wasn't pleasing the master and tightened his ass cheeks to demonstrate his total cooperation in being fucked.

"The price tag on that one is $800,000 U.S., John," Aristo said. "There aren't too many with natural good looks like that."

"He is a rare find, Aristo, and he takes his fucking well too. The price is high, but it's not as bad as I thought. I'll take him."

The slave being dildo-fucked was fully erect and dripping copiously from the prostate stimulation he was receiving with every stroke of the dildo. "Master," he gasped pleadingly, "Permission to shoot, master?"

"Go ahead, slave. I want to see your output anyway," his new owner commanded.

Immediately the boy bucked and heaved around the huge dildo jammed all the way in him and spewed load after load of steaming thick cum on the floor beneath him, some of it shot onto his stomach, chest, face, and legs in the process.

"God," John exclaimed, "I've bought a virtual cow. Jesus, there's cum everywhere," he remarked as his scooped some off of the slave's face and savored it in his mouth. "Nice tasting, though, and very creamy."

"He hasn't had a buyer look him over for quite some time now, so that's at least a two-week load there," Aristo laughed. "The handler will clean the mess up unless you want it bottled or you allow your new property to eat his cum - slaves trained here love to snack on their own cum as well as their master's. I think it's because it's a nice break from just eating slave chow all the time and they've learned to crave the taste as part of their training."

"Let's see, Aristo. Have the fitter put on a new collar with "Property of Morgan Enterprises, Ltd." along with his new name "Kansas." A bronze one would go well with his light tan color. A genital band, fitted real tight with a leash ring welded to the front, with the same engraving. Both tits ringed with very light one-inch trainer rings - just enough to agitate them into growing some - they're a little small right now for my taste - and, on this boy, bronze arm bands welded on above the biceps to emphasize his musculature."

"As good as done, John," Aristo said as he poked the instructions into his Palm Pilot. "You understand that's not suntan on the boy - that's his natural skin color. He's a quadroon."

"I figured as much," John said. "I like 'high yellows' myself. The build of the blacks with the fine features of a white in my opinion if the mix turns out right. Doesn't always, you know - some turn out patchy like and a few look runty."

"Some breeders are finding that out," Aristo commented. "They tell me they're getting one really superb quadroon for every three tries. That's really bad odds because the other three are just sold off as trash slaves for whatever they can get. Makes the successes like this boy all the more valuable, although this slave just happened - he wasn't bred or anything."

As "Kansas" licked up his own cum, the handler was already planning how to get all of Mr. Morgan's purchases caged and out to the yacht just as soon as this purchase was finished at the slavefitters with his new decorations.

———————

Sheik Tariq left soon afterward in that he wanted to be back in Dubai long before the chartered air transport arrived. He would need to supervise all the arrangements for moving them from the airstrip to his holding pens, filing the paperwork, and begin planning the subsequent sale of those purchased mainly to resell. John Morgan and he exchanged addresses and phone numbers in order to arrange the visit to Count Parsimi in Italy and, soon, go to John's estate in England to see the "Slavemobile" in action. The Sheik and Aristo again reiterated their intent to trade excess stock with each other and, toward that end, exchanged the fax numbers of their main slave handlers with each other. They already had each other's phone numbers, of course.

Two hours after Sheik Tariq's departure, John Morgan was back at the airstrip in Delos while his private jet was being loaded. Santos, dressed in his togs to drive the car to the airstrip, removed all of his clothing without being told and carefully folded it before beginning his work. Despite every possible configuration on Santos' part, only 10 cages could be fitted into the cargo department and the remaining cages had to stacked in the passenger compartment which filled it completely. John, piloting the plane, and Santos, now modestly dressed once again in his Delos outfit, sat in the pilot's cabin. Despite the heavy load, the jet took off the short airstrip fine and within five hours, they were landing at Morgan Enterprises' private landing strip at the Morgan estate. Santos deplaned with his new master, but, once out of the plane, with a nod from John Morgan, stripped completely and placed the neat outfit back in the pilot's compartment for the next trip. He then began unloading all of the cages as John called for a trunk to take the cages to the outside delivery area adjoining the slave quarters which now filled both the attic and the basement of his large manor house. By late afternoon, every new slave had been thoroughly scrubbed, douched, replugged, and penned. That night, John had two slaves in his own quarters: Santos whose body was being thoroughly enjoyed once again, and the new quadroon from Kansas who demonstrated just how well trained he was.

The next morning, John was on the telephone arranging for the engineer designing the slavemobile to take up permanent residence at the estate, now that the "power source" had been obtained to oversee the final construction of the contraption, the installation of the "engine" and to run test trials until it was perfected. The engineer was to be allowed full use of the "engine" slaves for his own enjoyment whenever he wanted as well as a healthy bonus if everything was completed within three weeks. The engineer had, of course, been chosen for his utmost discretion in matters of slavery - in fact, John had met him at an underground slave market in London where the engineer was busily trading in one slave on another fresh one, both Asian as John recalled.

Another call contacted Guilo Parsimi who was delighted to hear John had been able to purchase Santos and was eager to demonstrate his litter to Sheik Tariq as soon as possible. When John suggested he would like to deliver Santos and visit the Sheik in one trip, Guilo suggested they both be his house guests that weekend. John called Sheik Tariq and said the invitation for two days hence had been extended if that was possible with the Sheik's calendar. John would meet the Sheik at the Rome airport where Guilo's limousine would pick them up and take them on the one-hour trip to his villa. The Sheik immediately extended his thanks to John for arranging the visit and said he would make time for the visit to Italy.

Two days later, John, with Santos in his dress outfit heeling behind his master, met the sheik at the exclusive first class lounge for Emirates Air where they were informed that a Alfa Romeo limousine was awaiting them outside the nearest gate, Gate 22. With Santos carrying both men's luggage, they quickly found the rare model of Alfa. Sergei, fully dressed in an outfit almost identical to Santos, stood rigidly at attention by the back door. When he saw the masters approaching, he bowed deeply, his magnificent physique fully evident in the skin tight clothes he was wearing.

"Sergei, Sheik Tariq will be a guest of your master for a few days and the property with the luggage is my new slave handler, Santos. I'm sure the sheik will want to enjoy your body before I trade Santos for you on a long-term loan which I have arranged with your master. You'll be going back to England with me as my new slave handler and Santos will take over your duties here in Italy. You'll remain the property of Count Parsimi and Santos will remain my property. We're just loaning each other our properties for an indefinite period."

"I'll be leaving my master?" Sergei stammered out in total surprise.

"Temporarily, Sergei. I thought your master might have mentioned it in passing, but there's no need to mention anything to a slave, of course. At any rate, it's not a matter a slave is involved in. Your new duties will be similar to those here in Italy. I have a number of slaves who need a firm overseer and some organization of their time."

"Yes, master," Sergei said, quickly recovering from his shock. He didn't mind going with the good looking master from England who he knew well enough to suspect he would be a good master. It was just that he loved his Italian owner and hated being parted from him and he loved being a slave overseer, but the English master had mentioned continuing in that particular service.

After the Sheik and Mr. Morgan were comfortably seated in the limousine, Sergei inquired whether Mr. Morgan's slave should ride in the luggage compartment like most of the Count's slaves or if he should ride up front in the chauffeur's compartment.

"Up front with you, Sergei. After all, he'll have to learn to drive this monster before you go with me."

"Yes, master," both slaves said simultaneously as they quickly loaded the luggage and then hopped in the front compartment.

A hour later Santos had learned the idiosyncrasies of the Alfa limousine from his cohort and they were at the front entryway of the villa being greeted by Guilo.

"Sheik Tariq, John has spoken so highly of you," Guilo said. "I'm pleased you could visit my humble villa on such short notice. I've taken the liberty of arranging a litter ride for you later this afternoon after you've had a chance to relax and freshen up. You'll find two slaves in your guest quarters to do just that. John was kind enough to inform me of your preferences. You'll find a fine looking cold black slave from Nigeria and a handsome Latvian slave with blond hair and a magnificent build I hope you'll enjoy. They are both perfectly trained for your satisfaction, I hope, although the Latvian is a recent purchase. I'd appreciate your opinion of his performance, Sheik Tariq."

"John, I really appreciate your purchase of Santos," looking down at the Italian slave kneeling at his feet, tears streaming down the slave's face in his joy. "I feel guilty taking him from you so quickly, but I'm hoping you'll come to enjoy Sergei as much as I do."

The unexpected compliment of a mere slave left Sergei breathless and his master's acknowledgment led to a tear streaming down his own cheek.

"He's not only a very good overseer of the slaves here but, frankly, he's better in bed than any slave I've had other than Santos here. He's totally uninhibited and gives it everything he has exactly to your desires. Practically a perfect slave!" Guilo extolled.

"I hope I'm given the chance to compare the two slaves," Sheik Tariq laughed. "Sounds like you need an outside opinion on the slave's performance."

"Not tonight, Sheik," Guilo laughed. "I've waited too long to loan out Santos this early. But tomorrow at your convenience, I promise."

"Same for Sergei," John Morgan said. "I'll bed the Pole down tonight while you're playing around with the black and the blond. Tomorrow, you can have both of them at the same time, whatever's most convenient, so you can compare their performance, Hammad."

Without being told, Sergei and Santos had both stripped completely and neatly placed their clothes inside the luggage compartment of the car for now. Guilo took a leash out of his pocket and, with a nod of approval from the slave's owner, fastened it to Santos' collar while John did the same with Sergei. Out of nowhere seemingly, a huge handsome black slave and a striking blond slave appeared, leashes in hand, which they quickly handed to the Arabian guest before kneeling. The Sheik motioned for both of them to stand in display, leashed them by their genital rings, and let them led him, his luggage in their hands, to his guest suite, Santos and Sergei each heeled behind their new masters, growing hard as they anticipated what was forthcoming. Both were still crying silently in joy - one at being reunited with his long lost Italian master; the other at being publicly praised and appreciated.

All three masters were well satisfied with their bed mates that day. Each of the slaves involved tried their hardest to satisfy and succeeded quite well. By the time the huge litter appeared at the front entryway, the three were totally satiated and well pleased with the slaves assigned them.

The litter's baroque grandiosity took Sheik Tariq by surprise, but he, like all others, was most impressed with the naked, extremely muscular bearers chained by either their right or left tit to the litter itself. All, hugely hung, were fully erect. All were beautiful to look at - the very epitome of masculine strength and sexuality. Guilo and the Sheik climbed into the luxurious passenger compartment and with a simple command from Guilo, the litter was lifted smoothly onto the bearer's muscled shoulders and with another command of "Medium Pace," the litter moved gracefully forward faster and faster until each runner was at a full trot. Within minutes, the soft muted breathing of the bearers could be heard as they began rhythmically sucking air rapidly into their strained lungs and sweat covered their smooth naked skin. As they sped down the villa's many lanes, Guilo cracked his whip on the back of the lead slave with a sharp command: "Fast pace." The lead bearer howled as the whip slashed across his shoulders, but, instantly, the litter jolted forward. Guilo, continued lashing first one slave and then another until all had been motivated.

"This pace can only be maintained with a steady whip," Guilo explained as he continued lashing the slaves beneath him. "But the discipline and exertion is good for the slaves. We do a 'fast pace' routine every day. If I'm not around or in the mood, my overseer does it for me. Keeps the bearers in great shape and good wind, and, of course, slaves need discipline, especially draft slaves like this."

"I'll hardly call these magnificent properties 'draft slaves,' Count Parsimi. Where I live, such goods would be labeled 'premium,' he said admiringly as he watching the sweat soaked bodies strained to their utmost with their pricks still rock hard, their chained tits rapidly swelling and turning bright red in agitation from the heavy swinging tit leashes that attached them to the litter. "They're obviously beautifully trained," he continued as the litter sped ahead. "It's a very nice touch to have them in full erection at all times. That's quite a trick if I may say so. I take it you never let them unload to achieve the display?"

"They're milked every morning," Guilo laughed. "And either I or Sergei or my guests use them all the time. No, it's a matter of training. Sergei knows all the tricks. That's one reason John was willing to trade Santos for Sergei. He wants Sergei to train the black slaves he bought to power this 'slavemobile' contraption of his to be erect all the time - just like these slaves you see here."

"A nice touch. I can see John's reason now for being so generous in loaning you Santos, who, I must admit, is something else again when it comes to a 'turn-on' property. From what I've seen of him so far, John's right - he's just a natural whore, but, more important, he's the best looking whore in the world."

By this time in the journey, the litter bearers were gasping for air, sweat was raining off of their bodies, and the whip slashing across their backs and rumps was obviously necessary to keep up the fervent pace. Muted screams of pain couldn't be prevented as the whip tore into their shoulders and butt extracting the last ounce of effort from their bodies. But, eventually, the manor house was again in sight, and Guilo ordered the slaves to "Slow pace" and eventually "Halt" and then "Lower Litter" whereupon the slaves collapsed on the ground in a pool of sweat, lungs gasping, and muscles twitching with strain.

"I imagine John's slaves powering this 'slavemobile' contraption will look like this too after a good little trip around his estate, unless that engineer friend of his is a genius or something. But I think getting the most out of a slave is part of the fun, don't you, Sheik? Sort of a challenge?"

"Exactly," Sheik Tariq said. "It's the sport of the event that is most interesting and in this sport, it's getting slaves to produce everything they have. That's why I think John is going to enjoy his 'slavemobile.' It's as much sport as recreation."

"Yes, it's a little of both, all right, Sheik Tariq."

"Please call me Hammad and I'll call you Guilo," The sheik said warmly.

———————

Three days later, the Alfa was again whisking John and Hammad back to the Rome airport. Hammad had sampled the body of Santos thoroughly as well as Sergei had thoroughly enjoyed both the black and the Latvian furnished him, and had fucked anally and orally each and every one of Guilo's eight litter bearers. John had similarly indulged himself, but had screwed Santos over and over, knowing he might not see him again for some time. This time Santos, with a very sore ass and jaws aching from being stretched frequently, was driving the big car while Sergei, just as sore from overuse, sat next to him in the chauffeur's compartment. Both slaves looked as exhausted as their passengers in back.

"A wonderful experience," Sheik Tariq said finally. "Guilo has invited me again anytime I'm free and I intend to take him up on it. He can keep his silly litter, John, as far as I'm concerned, but the bearers - that's something else again. And his house staff is up to snuff too if that black and Latvian are any example. I couldn't get much beyond them - not enough time."

"All of Guilo's other slaves are just as good, believe me, Hammad. You can visit him ten times and always find something new. I always leave the villa just totally exhausted, if you know what I mean."

"Now I do, John," Hammad laughed. "We're much more laid back in Dubai - it's the heat I think, because we've got some interesting slaves on hand ourselves."

"Well, next stop and we'll be picked up at my airstrip in a very rough prototype of my 'slavemobile' if all is going on schedule. The engineer in charge called yesterday and said it was three weeks ahead of schedule: everything worked perfectly: all the parts went together in just a few hours; the blacks I bought, once they were put into their restraints, seemed to intuitively get the feel of the thing without two much blood letting, and the controls, which assures those blacks put out everything they have, have worked faultlessly. He claims he'll meet us at the airport and all three of us can ride back with a full load of luggage."

"What controls extracts the energy necessary from a mere six slaves to move three grown men and their luggage?"

"Well, he's using all eight as it turns out. Good thing I bought the whole lot when I did, because with just six, even those controls couldn't get the speed he wanted. But, the controls are basically an wireless electronic dildo jammed up their rear synchronized with the accelerator, an electronic pain shock device attached to their collars, and tight leashes on those collars, their genitals and their tits so there is no way they can move out of position. Once fastened in, all they can do is run on that treadmill like their life depended on it. A few moments with a shock collar on as well as a electric dildo up you and you believe your life depends on it. Those dildos and collars can deliver shocks just short of tissue damage and even then, you'll sometimes get some burn marks up their butts or around their necks after a particularly demanding outing. It's something Sergei can take care - he's good at managing stock."

The three men had an uneventful trip in John's jet back to the English estate where Sheik Tariq explained his new arrangements with Guiliano Imports. The exchange of excess stock had been agreed upon with 20% discounts applied to any and all exchange properties so that the privilege wasn't overused. The Tariq family breeding farm, located in an isolated location in the Emirates, would produce exclusively for Guiliano Imports (as well as the Tariq family) to specification: orders would be placed and approximately 18 to 19 years later the finished product was delivered fully trained and ready for sale. Guiliano Imports would get a 40% discount from current market prices if they paid a 10% non-returnable deposit on future goods at the time of placing the order. Anything could be ordered to specification: gender, skin color, physique size, musculature, size of sex organs, hair color, eye color, etc. The arrangement was favorable to both parties: the Tariq family got working capital up front and a guaranteed market for their products; Guiliano Imports could speculate in commodities trading - in effect, placing bets on what would bring top prices in the market 15 to 20 years down the line. Tariq's studs and brood mares could be kept busy around the clock to meet demands; Guiliano Imports would get a steady supply of new stock acclimated to their status.

Once they arrived, sure enough, the 'slavemobile' was waiting just where the plane was tied down. The slaves, still gleaming in sweat from the run out to the airstrip but breathing normally by this time, were exactly positioned as the engineer had described. The collars, with the shock devices attached, were short-leashed to a holding bar extending on both sides for each set of slaves, right and left, on the treadmills. Their tits were similarly short leashed to the holding bar so no movement of the upper torso was possible without serious pain to the tits. Below, each genital band was short leashed to another holding bar lower down on each side, again assuring that any untoward movement by the slave would lead to instant tugging on the slave's balls and considerable pain. In each slave's tightly positioned rump could be seen the 'antennae' of their wireless dildo shocker, controlled by the accelerator up front. More speed, more shock; less speed, less shock. The shock collar was connected to the brakes wirelessly: a jolt to the collar indicated braking; the harder the jolt, the more braking necessary. The matched set of eight slaves were most impressive in their restraints and really looked splendid as part of the overall configuration. It was a picture of total dominance by those owning slaves; a picture of total subservience on the part of the owned; and a preview of how far slave power could be extended into everyday usage. For connoisseurs of human flesh, the tightly constrained magnificent paragons of masculinity was a work of art. Both John and the Sheik knew, in that first moment, that the 'slavemobile' would be a sensation when introduced to the discriminating slave owner and marketing it would be simple: it would simply sell itself in that everyone able to afford eight strong slaves would have to have one within the privacy of their own private estates and secluded hideaways around the world.

"You've got a winner here," Sheik Tariq said as they stepped in for the first ride. "I'm placing my order for one right now."

"Wait until Guilo sees it!" John exclaimed as he pressed down on the accelerator and the 'slavemobile' smoothly glided forward despite the heavy load. The only sound, faint since it was far in the back, was the slave's gasping for air and the muted moans as the dildos motivated them deep inside their bodies. When they quickly arrived at the manor house, John applied the brakes and the sounds of choked screams of pain indicated the shock collars were working beautifully. Stepping out, John said, "You want to take it for a solo spin now, Hammad? There's nothing to it, really."

Hammad took him up on the offer and the gasping, sweating slaves in the rear had barely recovered their breath before the dildo summoned them to action again. By the time Hammad returned, the slaves looked to be exhausted but dared not change their position due to their potentially painful restraints.

"Beautiful! When can I expect delivery?" he enthused as he exited.

"You'll be the first, Hammad. And Guilo will probably be the second. Once he takes this for a spin, he'll dump that old Roman litter in a moment. Hell, he's already got the energy pack for it, so all he needs is the contraption itself."

Once back in the Manor House, John showed Hammad the three house slaves he was assigning to Tariq's suite during his short stay.

"You'll recognize them, Hammad," John laughed. "They're all products of the Tariq Breeding Farm which I bought at Guiliano Imports fully trained for an average price of $400,000," as the three slaves stood in full display position and turned slowly so the foreign guests, once their master, could see all aspects of their handsome, muscular, and very hung bodies."

"The first one here," John said as he hefted the beautiful black slave's genitals in his hand, "is just 19. You'd bred him from American Black stock to the exact specifications of Guiliano Imports. He's pleasuring 10 to 12 guests a day currently, and even though he's just 19 now, he'll probably need to be sold off in his mid-20s due to his usage rate. But you can see why. He's pretty enough to eat," as the beautifully muscled slave, fully erect, gave the Sheik an inviting smile.

"This second one," John said as he moved to the next slave and inserted a finger up the slave's hole for emphasis, "is 25, and is one of the 'slavemobile' team. That's why he's so incredibly muscular - all that training for the machine. His duties here in the manor house is so easy by comparison to working on the 'slavemobile' that he puts everything he has into pleasing those selecting him for use. Guests liking the very muscular take to the 'slavemobile' crew, and, as you noticed, the entire crew is very good looking. But we'll sell him off in five years max - he'll be pretty well worn out by then," John added as he pumped his finger in and out of the slave's asshole to demonstrate the slave's ready compliance in taking a good fucking

"This third slave," John said as he moved to the last slave 'given' to the Sheik for his amusement, "is a mixed blood slave - he's half American Black and half Royal Hansa - one of the Tariq Breeding Farm's most successful blendings in my opinion, Sheik. He's very popular with the manor house's discriminating guests who keep the slave, let me tell you, mighty busy in their beds."

"How long do you keep slaves like this around," Sheik Tariq asked languidly as he began stroking the huge equipment on the member of the 'slavemobile' crew being shown.

"In another four or five years, all three slaves here will be sold off, or given as gifts, to favored friends and business partners of Morgan Enterprises and replaced by fresh stock, Hammad."

"And are all your houseboys black?" Hammad asked with a little laugh.

"The Morgan houseboys are typically black stock due to my own personal preferences and their ability to hold up under heavy usage as well as, Hammad, their excellent resale value. In my opinion, if these boys are any sample, your arrangement between Guiliano Imports and the Tariq Breeding Farm will be extremely profitable as well as insure a steady supply of slaves like this for generations to come."

"That's exactly what both Ernesto Guiliano and I have in mind, John," Sheik Tariq laughed, "although we offer a full range of colors, sizes, and shapes to meet the preferences of all types of customers. But I do thank you for these bed bucks, John. They're mighty attractive if I do say so myself, having bred them, and I like to bed down blacks every now and then although most of mine at home, as you know, are blond boys. But variety is good for the soul as they say," as the black being stroked begin dripping copiously and began struggling to control a pending eruption.

"I just may equip my 'slavemobile' with a crew like this," Sheik Tariq said. "I've got the stock at the Breeding Farm and Ernesto Guiliano can train them for me in four or five months."

"Sounds great, Hammad. Enjoy!" he said, pointing to the three slaves as he said good night to his good friend. "Breakfast at 10 AM, in the solarium."

SIX MONTHS LATER:

"John, Ernesto Guiliano here," the deep bass voice resonated over the phone. "Sorry to bother you, but you asked for first option on that British construction worker - you know, that rogue slave with a ring in his nose you traded in on some new stock some time ago - once he had been broken and properly trained."

"Thanks for calling, Ernesto," John replied pleasantly. "I appreciate it. At the time I traded him in, as I told you, I didn't think there was any way on God's earth you could train that bastard into anything sellable. I take it you had some degree of success?"

"We've never failed to properly train a slave yet, John," Ernesto laughed, "although this one did take six months to reach our standards instead of the usual four. But now, you'd never know he had ever once been a free man, let alone one about as rebellious to being turned into a slave as I've ever seen. Some Brits are tough nuts to crack, but crack they do eventually."

"Do you still have to leash him by his nose ring to get him to mind?" John asked jokingly. "I remember I had to short-leash him by his nose to the bars of his cage to even get him down to your island without risking life and limb."

"Your life or his?" Ernesto laughed.

"Both," John jocularly replied.

"Well, the nose ring is gone, at least for now. Our sales department thought it detracted from his appearance and, of course, it's no longer needed for control purposes. Actually, John, we've prettied him up considerably."

"How so?" John asked.

"Well, a complete body shave helped considerably - he was mighty hairy if you recall and all that bush was hiding some of his best assets. Now he's hairless below the neck. The only hair the boy has is his head hair, a handsome pencil-line beard to emphasize his jaw line, and those long eye lashes and thick eyebrows. He's completely muscled now - our exercise program has done its usual thorough job of perfecting a slave's physique. We've trimmed him - you remember he wasn't circumcised - so that big thick penis is fully exposed now and his tight genital band around those big balls of his makes sure he displays well at all times, especially since we control his outlets so he shows hard most of the time anymore. Both of his tits are about three times bigger than when you last saw him due to the heavy tit rings we've permanently installed. And a very tall heavy neck collar makes sure his handsome facial features are easily visible at all times - the slave can't bend his head down anymore so he's learned to display his face as proudly as he shows off that huge package between his legs. We took out the nose ring once he was fully trained in that we thought it detracted from his good looks, but a new owner could put one back in an instance - the hole in his septum is still there, of course, right where you first fitted him. He's fully tanned all over and is trained to give his body a nice coating of pine-scented body oil for sheen after every cleansing, right after he lubes his hole. His hair is shoulder length now and shampooed every day - we thought its luster and fine texture was one of the slave's best features and he's so masculine otherwise, the long hair only enhances his manliness."

"I thought he was a looker when I first bought him off that London slave catcher, but it sounds like you've turned him into something worth looking at," John commented. "But, pretty or not, I remember him screaming and squalling every single time you poked something up his ass as if you were killing him, squirming and bucking so you could hardly manage to properly rape him."

"Well, such silliness is long forgotten by now," Ernesto said soothingly. "Just this morning I watched a potential buyer fuck him for a good hour or so as a try-out and, John, you'll find this hard to believe, but the slave was enjoying it as much as the buyer judging by the way he was moaning in ecstasy and dripping from his hard cock the whole time. The buyer told me that once he was well up the slave's chute, the Brit pumped him with his ass muscles so thoroughly he didn't have to piston the slave at all - the slave literally did all the work for him! And, John, that buyer was hung as heavy as the slave he was fucking - that old construction worker took the entire 13" up his ass without a murmur of protest or resistance even though that buyer was about as thick as they come as well as super long."

"How does he suck?" John asked. "The last time I tried to force face-fuck him, he tried to bite and by the time I had knocked some sense into him, he was unconscious so I never could try him out that way."

"He doesn't just suck you off, John. This slave deep throats you all the way down so his throat muscles massage your dick on all sides and you spell your load directly into his stomach. Even that buyer with the phenomenal dick was shocked when he took a 13x6 incher all the way down with only a few minor gags and just a little choking. The Brit's mouth was stretched like it was going to split at the seams and you could see the outline of that big dick in his throat, but he never once faltered until the buyer had shot a big load down into his stomach and was fully drained. And, you know, John, the slave thanked his user for that big load with such sincerity there were practically tears in his eyes. It was like he hadn't be fed in a week, but all slaves waiting to be sold get mouth action at least twice a day - just to keep them in practice if nothing else - and, of course, they do like feeding on cum to break the monotony of their regular chow."

"Ernesto, if I may ask, who's the buyer that's interested?" John asked.

"You've met him, John," Ernesto laughed. "Aristo told me he was here when you last visited and you didn't care for him much. An

American dealer from Texas that Aristo said you called obnoxious. Aristo told me he didn't like him much either, but sales are sales and we'll sell the Brit to him if the price is right. I'll say one thing for him - his prick is as big as his mouth. If he buys the Brit, that slave going to be fucked half to death before he's resold to some customer of the dealer down in Texas. But, of course, that's what we train slaves to expect. After all, that's why most people buy slaves anyway - especially slaves looking as great as the Brit."

"Well, of course, Ernesto. That's what I would do myself if the slave is truly broken and fully trained now."

"He is, John. You can trust me on that one. We can even give you a 60-day guarantee if that would make you feel better," Ernesto laughed. "You can fuck this slave continuously if you want and all the slave will do, other than possibly die in the process, is thank you for using him with cum dripping out of his prick the whole time. But the slave has other uses as well: he's so muscular you could use him on this 'slavemobile' contraption you're so proud of with no problems; he'd make a great display slave for you to show off to your friends; and, if you want, you could whore him out to your guests with no problem at all. And, you know what, John? I think he would make a great slave overseer. Slaves that took a while to break to their new status and took a lot of training tend to make the best trainers and overseers. They seem to understand all a slave's little tricks of resisting total compliance and pretending they're broken when in fact they're aren't. It's like they always say: 'You can fool an owner occasionally, but never a true slave.' John, the Brit is a true slave now if there ever was one. You could give him his freedom tomorrow and he'd be miserable, begging you to take him back as your property. Once fully broken, there's no going back."

"I've heard that, but never understood why," John mused.

"Once all your needs are met by others and all decision making is removed from your life, it's addictive. You can't give it up once you've experienced it. A slave's life is all they can live once they've settled in."

"You mean that's the only way they can be happy and satisfied?" John asked.

"Exactly," Ernesto said. "Think about it. You and I would be just like that if we were trained like our slaves here."

"What's my option?" John asked.

"You can buy the Brit fully trained if you're willing to meet the best offer we can get on him. We guaranteed you that when you traded the Brit in on all that new stock you purchased."

"The Texan has made an offer, I suppose?" John asked.

"Yes, $800,000 U.S. dollars plus shipment costs."

"I'll take him if you throw in the 60-day money-back guarantee you mentioned," John said. "I need another slave like a hole in the head, but I'm intrigued with the fact I knew the slave before he was really a slave - it will make ownership all the more enjoyable."

"You'll get your guarantee, John, although I can assure you you'll never be bringing this slave back for retraining," Ernesto laughed. "As it turned out, the rebellious rogue was a natural born slave if there ever was one - he just needed some serious training to reveal his true character. That's why he always excited and dripping - he loves being used by others for their pleasure. Here's a boy that loves to be owned. For him, it's love. That's what marks a natural slave even more than their ownership brands. Which reminds me, how do you want him fitted?"

"Keep the genital band and the tall collar and the tit rings on him - they all sound good. I assume he's properly branded with the Guiliano Imports logo. But for old times sake, reinstall his nose ring, but this time a small one that doesn't cover his lips - I love leading slaves around by a leash to a nose ring and a small ring shouldn't ruin his good looks. And I think a couple of arm bands above his biceps and both ankles banded would be a nice touch - all in the same metal as his neck collar and genital band so it all matches."

"Is that the way you fit your 'slavemobile' properties now?" Ernesto asked.

"No, Ernesto. I doubt if I'll use this slave for that. I plan to use him as a personal bed buck until I tire of him, and then I'm going to sell him to a black American billionaire who loves having a bevy of white slave boys available at all times. He'll pay plenty to get a good looking, fully trained Brit in his bed. He's asked me to be on the lookout for a handsome British slave."

"We'll have him fitted, cleaned out, drugged and shipped out express air tomorrow in our usual soundproof cages that look like shipping crates. Your new property should arrive no later than 4 PM your time tomorrow. The drug will have worn off by 7 or 8 PM so you can start full use of him tomorrow night. I assume you will wire us a bank draft before we ship him out?"

"I'll get the money electronically transferred as soon as we hang up - no problem. I have your bank's transfer number in my computer."

"When you uncage him tomorrow afternoon and he wakes up fully, you're not going to recognize him at first, John. He's really a looker now - exceptional if I do say so myself. It's hard to remember the scrumpy rebellious rogue - all hairy with piss and cum all over him screaming obscenities - that you traded in six months ago. This shiny beauty thanks you for fucking him and dreams up new ways to bring his owner pleasure. It's a testament to our training methods if I do say so myself. I'm really proud of this final outcome."

"Self praise is no praise at all," John laughed. "But I'm willing to take your word for it. If you're not right, I want my money back. If you are right, I've got some interesting new meat for my bed and a little profit to be made selling the bastard to that black kingpin in America who likes to collect handsome white slave boys."

"To each their own," Ernesto laughed. "That's what keeps us in business."

ABOUT THE AUTHOR

Bill Smith is a prolific writer of various fantasy tales about slaves and the huge variety of fictional societies and settings that foster them.

Bill Smith is also the author of *Bates Training Center* and *The Brazilian*. Available at Amazon.com, TheNazcaPlainsCorp.com or your local bookstore.

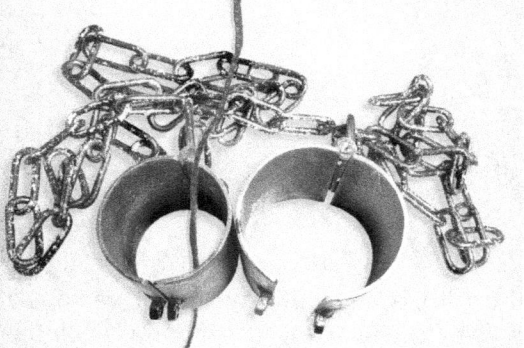

BATES
TRAINING CENTER

A NOVEL BY
BILL SMITH

A
BONER
BOOK

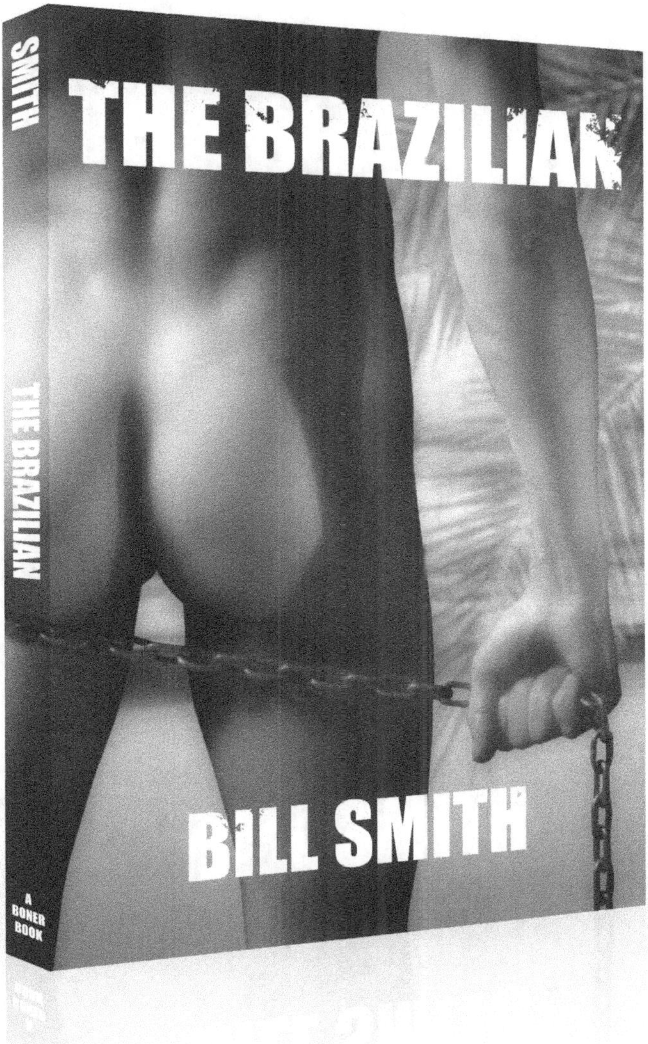
THE BRAZILIAN
BILL SMITH
SMITH
THE BRAZILIAN
A BONER BOOK

www.ingramcontent.com/pod-product-compliance
Lightning Source LLC
Chambersburg PA
CBHW051131260626
47170CB00005B/1766